A Spot of Tea

ANJ Press

Pittsburgh

A SPOT OF TEA

ANJ Press, First edition. July 2024.

Copyright © 2024 Amelia Addler.

Written by Amelia Addler.

Cover design by Lori Jackson
https://www.lorijacksondesign.com/

Maps by MistyBeee

for sisters,
especially mine

Recap and Introduction to
A Spot of Tea

Welcome back to San Juan Island, Washington! In our last story, Sheila Dennet moved to the island to help her feisty mother-in-law Patty keep her seaside tea shop afloat.

A recent empty nester and the mother of four daughters, Sheila had a lot to discover about herself – her strength, her passion for performing music, and her appeal to neighbor Russell Westwood, retired Hollywood star.

With Russell's help, Sheila was able to right a wrong from her past. Years prior, her fisherman father had captured, and subsequently sold off, an orca whale calf named Lottie.

In *A Spot of Tea*, Russell and Sheila continue the project of moving Lottie out of the amusement park where she's lived for decades and into a retirement sea pen near San Juan Island.

Eliza also stays on to help run the tea shop, and finds herself caught up in a romance of her own...

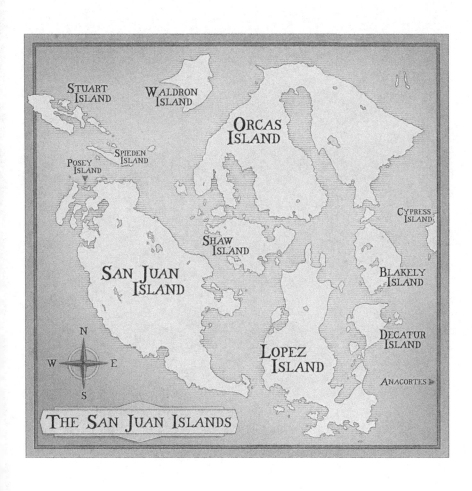

One

Getting unstuck is no small task, and Eliza was never more aware of that fact as she unpeeled last year's tax return from a sheet with her old SAT results.

She tugged, and the SAT paper gave way first, a hole tearing just above the spot where her score was listed: **1550**.

"Almost perfect," her dad had said when he saw it.

Had that been eight years ago? Or nine? When she was still a bright-eyed high school student, her life spread out ahead of her like a web of invisible opportunities.

She dropped the tax return on top of her college transcript. Five semesters completed. Five years since she'd dropped out.

Five years *stuck*.

Her life didn't have endless, branching possibilities anymore. With each passing year, the potential future lives fell away, their hollow tree limbs crashing to the ground and splintering to dust at her feet.

Eliza picked up the pile of papers. She wasn't going to live in a forest of her mistakes. Her legs weren't stuck in the ground. All she needed was initiative, and she would get herself unstuck.

Or at least she'd cause a *lot* of trouble, which sometimes, was the same thing.

It was a blessing, really, that Eliza didn't see any of it coming. If she had, she may never have left the house at all.

She couldn't stand any delay. Eliza couldn't even imagine eating breakfast, her stomach flipping as she descended the stairs, the scent of frying butter filling her nostrils.

Granny Patty didn't notice her until she opened the front door.

"Wait!" She called out from the kitchen. "I'm making omelets!"

"Sorry, Granny. I have to run to the bank before opening the tea shop." Eliza held onto the doorknob, her breaths hitching against the nausea building in her core. "I'll eat when I get back."

She slipped outside. The cool April air filled her lungs and stilled her stomach. Sunrise was well under way, and the ocean sparkled blindingly as she got into her car.

I guess it's a nice place to run away from your problems...

Her dad's voice kept popping into her head like a catchy song. She sighed and started the engine.

He was the spark for all this upheaval. Eliza had been happy. The work she'd put into Granny's tea shop was paying off. They were bringing in new customers, sending out orders. Eliza had been able to save a little bit of money.

Then, it happened again, that unwanted day that marked her life for all to see.

Her birthday.

Her dad had called early that morning. "I'm glad you're having fun, Eliza, but you're twenty-five. You're growing up. Are you planning to work at that tea shop forever?"

She'd laughed, as she'd learned to do whenever her heart was punctured. "Of course not."

It wasn't his fault for stating the obvious. If it weren't true, it wouldn't have hurt. She couldn't blame him for her decision to drop out of school and lose her full-ride scholarship.

How was he supposed to know about the deep well of shame she kept locked in her soul? After all, she kept it covered with jokes and movie quotes. It was better camouflaged than a nest of baby rabbits in the spring, and far less adorable.

Eliza pulled into the parking lot of Pebble Bay Bank. She probably should have made an appointment, but the last time she'd done that, she couldn't bring herself to go inside.

This time, she was doing it on the fly, before she could practice answering the questions the loan officer would be too polite to ask. "Why would you drop out? Do you even have a plan for your life?"

Eliza shut off her car. There was no point imagining conversations. No one cared about her personal life. This wasn't a morality center. It was a bank. The opposite of moral, historically speaking.

She got out of the car, straightened her shoulders, and stopped. A white pickup truck stood in front of the bank, blocking the ATM, its back tire lifted onto the sidewalk.

Eliza edged toward it, following the sound of grunting until she saw a man wheeling himself in a wheelchair. He stopped at the cab of the truck, tugging at the strap of a bag.

"Ridiculous," he muttered as the bag fell onto his lap and onto the ground.

"Hey, would you like a hand?" Eliza asked, peering around the truck.

"Huh?" He startled, squinting at her from under the brim of his cowboy hat. The brown wool was worn light at the edges, and a pink-and-gold tasseled band encircled the cap.

His voice was muffled by a blue surgical mask. "Do I what now?"

She shouldn't have stopped him. He was busy. He didn't want to be bothered by her.

But now she had to explain herself. "Um, sorry! Just making sure you didn't want any help with that."

He grunted and looked down at the bag on the sidewalk, then back at her, the tassel on his hat swinging wildly with each motion, the gold thread catching in the sun. "You know, that's not a bad idea. You think you can get my bags for me?"

She let out a breath. "Yes, of course!"

"There's another bag in the back," he said, pointing.

Eliza stooped to pick up the black duffel bag from the ground, slung the strap over her shoulder, and stood slowly under the weight. She reached over and lifted the book bag from the truck with her free hand.

"You can give me that one," he said, taking it from her with a swift pull.

"Are you headed inside?" The strap cut into her shoulder. She shifted the weight.

"Yeah. Just popping in, if you don't mind."

"Not at all." She smiled at him. He didn't notice. "That's where I'm going, too."

The automatic doors threw themselves open and he wheeled himself inside, the book bag on his lap.

Eliza followed, walking into a wall of smells as she crossed the threshold – coffee, lemon-scented cleaning solution, and the sickly sweetness of donuts caked in powdered sugar.

She put a hand on her stomach. Turning, turning. Maybe skipping breakfast hadn't been such a good idea after all.

Two tellers chatted, oblivious to their arrival, and a third woman seated in a cubicle glanced up at them before looking back and tapping speedily at her keyboard. Next to her was a silver frame with two smiling, gap-toothed faces.

Eliza took a deep breath. That might be the loan officer – a woman with a full life. Kids. Emails. Suits to dry clean. She had better things to do than judge Eliza's bad choices. It was going to be okay.

"Do me a favor," the man said in a low voice. "Dump that bag onto the floor."

She looked at him. "Like, drop it?"

"Unzip it and dump what's inside of it out," he said. "I'm paying back a loan with pennies and dimes and I'd like to make a dramatic entrance."

She'd heard of people doing that before. It seemed petty, but who was she to judge? "Oh, sure."

She knelt and the bag hit the floor with a thud. Eliza unzipped the top and tipped it forward. A black box fell out, its surface adorned with wires, blinking red and green lights, and a large, bright clock, the time ticking down in red.

She turned her head, trying to process what she was looking at. Was it a piggy bank, maybe? A lockbox? "Are the coins in there?"

The man jumped from his wheelchair, landing on his feet. "Everyone listen up. This will only take a second!"

The room fell silent and Eliza sat on the floor, her face inches away from his cowboy boots.

"I've got a bomb here with a deadman's switch. This is a robbery. If it's your first, welcome!"

The empty bag lay next to her, flat and lifeless. She scrambled backwards and slammed her head into the cubicle wall, sending it rocking.

"Hey!" the robber barked, pointing at her.

She shot straight up, her hands in the air, her chest tight.

"Not so fast," he said. "No sudden movements and no phone calls. You get me? I'm trying to make some money here."

His face shimmered and sparkled in front of her, and Eliza nodded, both hands over her mouth. She sucked in a breath just as the ground lurched beneath her and the bright lights faded to total darkness.

Two

It had been two weeks since the bank robbery, and people thought they were *so* clever, torturing poor Eliza about it.

After a group of three young men strutted into the tea shop that morning, Patty never took her eyes off them. What teenage boys wanted tea and crumpets at nine in the morning?

She'd been right to stare them down. As soon as they'd eaten their plate of chocolate chip cookies, the ringleader boy, the one with the constant smirk, pulled out his phone and started playing a video with *the song*.

Oh, Patty hated that song. Some goober on the internet thought it would be cute to take the security footage of Eliza fainting at the bank and set techno music to it. They had added in a scream and a laugh track and now everyone kept playing it like it was the funniest thing since George Carlin.

Patty ripped off her apron, muttering to herself. "The three of you don't add up to a *single* George."

She had only taken one step before a hand landed on her shoulder. "Now hang on."

It was her boyfriend Reggie and his gentle, even-paced tone.

"You know Eliza doesn't like bringing attention to it. She told you to stop yelling at people. Said you don't understand how the internet works, and it'll ruin your reputation as the Cute Tea Granny."

"I don't give a hoot about my reputation," Patty snapped. "I care about them playing that *stupid* song loud enough for her to hear!"

It would be one thing if the song had stayed on the internet, but no. Instead, it had made the rounds.

The local news had featured it. Then the late-night talk shows had picked it up. And now brats had brought it into the tea shop, trying to catch her reaction on camera!

Eliza never said a word—just smiled, blushed, and darted away.

It was downright cruel and Patty was sick of it.

"How about you take a walk outside and cool down?" Reggie said. "I'll go over to the table and start a conversation with them. I'll bore them into leaving."

"Like that's going to work," Patty snapped, but she knew he was right, and he was already leading her to the door.

He gave her a kiss on the cheek and sent her out into the sunshine.

The sea stared back at her, an endless blue wall of calm. It could teach her a wise lesson about rolling with the waves, but she wasn't having it. Wisdom was useless when it came to someone she loved being hurt.

She walked down to the water and spied her neighbor Russell standing at his shore, talking to a young man.

Now *there* was an idea. Patty smiled and walked over.

"Joey, isn't it?" she asked, inserting herself into their conversation.

"Morning, Patty. Nice to see you," Russell said with his easy movie star smile.

It was fun to have a movie star as a neighbor. Even more fun since he'd started dating her daughter-in-law Sheila, just like she'd hoped he would.

Not hoped. *Knew.* In her eighty-one years on this earth, she'd learned a thing or two, even if no one wanted to admit it.

"Hi," Joey said, sticking out his hand. "It's nice to meet you."

Patty smiled and shook his hand. "You're Russell's new pilot, right?"

She was being polite. She knew exactly who he was. She'd heard Sheila rant about how wasteful it was to buy a seaplane and hire a pilot – and she'd heard Russell's charming, laughter-filled counter arguments.

Both of them were fully committed to building a sea pen for Lottie the orca. Russell had worked with the researchers to secure an old fishing lodge on Stuart Island, and now they were completely rebuilding it.

Sheila did her part, keeping an eye on the money, and though she was good at it, Russell's flair for the dramatic some-times won out.

The pilot got to stay, and Patty had never been more glad for it. "How old are you?"

"Who wants to know?" Joey asked with a dashing smile.

He looked about Eliza's age, though Patty wasn't sure. Anyone under fifty looked like a kid to her. He was at least young enough to know how the internet worked.

"He's a qualified pilot, don't worry," Russell said. "Would you like to go for a flight?"

"No, thank you," Patty said simply. "How would you like to make twenty-five dollars, Joey?"

He glanced at Russell. "Should I worry about the legality of how I'd make these twenty-five dollars?"

"Of course not." Patty stepped closer and lowered her voice. "Don't look at him. Look at me."

Joey, wide-eyed, glanced at Russell.

"Listen to her," Russell said, putting his hands up. "I can't protect you from her."

"Did you hear about the bank robbery in town?" Patty asked.

Joey scratched the back of his neck. "Uh, yes. Of course."

Russell laughed, opening his mouth to say something, but Patty pressed on.

"My granddaughter Eliza was there when it happened. She ended up on the security footage, and it's turned into a big joke for people, coming to the tea shop to ridicule her."

Joey's smile faded. "That's not nice."

Patty pointed at the tea shop over the hill. "I will give you twenty-five dollars if you go in there and get that table of hooligans to stop bullying her."

Russell shrugged. "How about this, Patty? I'll do it for free."

"Oh shush! You would only bring more notoriety, Mr. Hollywood." She turned to Joey. "What do you say? Twenty-five dollars. No violence, of course, but threats...might be useful."

He laughed. "Threats. Right."

Patty wasn't sure if she had that much in her purse. It might only be twenty. Or maybe just five. It didn't matter. The money was just to get his interest.

Russell grinned and clapped his hands together. "Are you sure I can't be part of it? I never get to threaten people anymore."

"I didn't ask you, Russell!" Patty shot him a glare, then turned to Joey. "What do you say?"

"I think I can help." He nodded. "Yeah, I'd be happy to try."

Patty smiled. "Good. Follow me."

Three

The hill to the teashop was steeper than Joey had expected, or perhaps Patty was faster than she looked. He followed her, sucking gulps of salted air, staring up at the light blue sky.

The robbery wasn't news to him. He couldn't go anywhere on the island without overhearing someone blathering on that if they'd been there, the robber wouldn't have stood a chance at getting away.

The bluster was only going to get worse. Just that morning, Pebble Bay Bank had announced a one-hundred-thousand-dollar reward to anyone who provided information leading to the arrest of the robber.

No one had been able to identify the guy, even after he'd hit thirteen banks. Patty's grandkid was the only one who had spoken to him outside of his robbing commands.

The tea shop sat at the top of the hill, the paint a pale sea foam green and the windows framed in white. Outside, tables sat empty, their umbrellas rocking in their bases.

"Are you coming?" Patty asked, looking over her shoulder.

He nodded and rushed forward. It couldn't hurt to talk to the kid. He might learn something, and it'd be his good deed for the day.

They stood at the front door, her hand on the doorknob. "You'll see them. They're the only ones in there. I'm not supposed to get involved, but…"

She let out a huff and shook her head.

"I understand," Joey said. "Nobody likes a bully."

She opened the door and a pair of bells jingled merrily.

Joey walked in, surveying the small space. *Jagged* by Old 97's played softly in the background, and in the far room he spotted a table with a trio of young teenage boys giggling over a cell phone.

Patty scowled, pointing at an older man seated at the table. He stood and met them in the small lobby.

"It isn't working," he said with a sigh.

"I can see that," she said through clenched teeth. "Help me in the kitchen, Reg."

She cast a brief smile at Joey before disappearing behind a swinging door.

A snort rang out from the table, followed by the loud thumping of a bass-heavy song.

Joey sighed. He remembered being a teenage boy. He had not been his best self then.

He walked over to the table and pulled out a chair. "What're you guys listening to?"

The boy with the phone shot him a glance. "Nothing."

"C'mon. What is it?"

"It's a song," one of the boys offered. "From the robbery."

"What robbery?"

The first boy spoke again, his eyes and lips twisted in disbelief. "Didn't you hear about the bank robbery in town?"

Joey sat back and looked up at the ceiling. "Huh, no. I'm not from around here. I'm a pilot, just flew into town."

The boy with the phone shot a heavy glance at his friends. "Oh yeah?"

"Seaplanes," he said with a nod.

The boy glanced at his friends. "What do you fly on the planes?"

"People. Things." Joey shrugged. "You've got a video of the guy who robbed the bank?"

The boy's eyes grew wide and he tucked the phone into his hoodie pocket. "No, it's just of this lady screaming and fainting. When she was there."

"Fainting?" Joey leaned in and lowered his voice. "She saw him, then? Do you know who this lady is?"

All three boys instantly said, "No."

"Huh." Joey sat back and crossed his arms. "Too bad."

"Uh, we've got to get going." The boy tucked away his phone and stood.

The other two stood, nodding. "Yeah."

"Let me know if you need to fly anywhere!" Joey yelled. "Or rob any banks!"

They ran, pushing each other, their laughter carrying until the door shut it out.

Mission accomplished.

The rumor of the bank robber escaping the island by seaplane had reached these boys, it seemed. That wasn't good.

Joey stood from his seat as someone emerged from the swinging door. Her long hair was pulled into a ponytail over her right shoulder, her black-rimmed glasses sitting high on her nose.

He stopped. Patty's grandchild wasn't actually a child. She was an adult woman – and a pretty one, too.

Maybe there was more to this tea shop than unruly kids.

Joey gawked at her gliding through the tea shop, a black apron tied around her waist. She stopped when she reached him.

"Thanks for that," she said, smiling as she loaded a tray with cups and plates. "They'd paid almost an hour ago but refused to leave."

"No problem. They seemed like they were up to no good." He cleared his throat and thrust out his hand. "I'm Joey, by the way. Russell's new pilot."

"Oh!" She wiped her hand on her apron before shaking his. "I've heard so much about you."

He raised an eyebrow. "All good things?"

She laughed, reaching to gather the last plate from the table. "It wasn't *bad*, exactly. My mom, Sheila, is Russell's accountant. She's also his girlfriend, but that's another story." She stood, balancing the tray on her hip. "She didn't think Russell's idea to hire a full-time pilot was the most economical decision."

"Ah." Joey smiled. "No, she's right. I'm a horrible waste of money."

She put a hand up. "No! I don't – that's not what I meant. She was hesitant *at first,* but she said you've been so helpful with getting people to the sea pen site and dealing with some of the divas coming through."

He nodded. "Yeah, those whale researchers really expect the red carpet rolled out for them."

She laughed again. "Right. *Them.*"

He knew what she meant. There was a certain pop singer who had thought she could show up and secure a photo-op by the sea pen site without actually being involved. Joey had flown her around the island for an hour until she agreed to at least make a donation.

"Can I get you a menu?" she asked.

Joey slipped into a nearby seat and smiled up at her. "Yes, please. And your name when you have a chance."

She frowned. "Oh, sorry. I'm Eliza."

"Eliza. Nice to meet you."

"I'll be back to get your order."

She disappeared through the swinging door. He pulled out his phone and searched **Pebble Bay bank robberies.**

A video with edited security footage popped up – **FAINT AND FURIOUS: HILARIOUS BANK ROBBERY REACTION!**

"Here's the menu." She handed him a thick spiral-bound booklet. "You'll find information about all of our teas, and on this page, we have our food specials."

Joey tucked his phone away. "Thanks." He paused. "Those kids were trying to tease you about the bank robbery, right?"

"They tried, but the joke is on them."

He set the menu down. "Oh yeah?"

"Five months ago, a red car with damage to the rear bumper was spotted doing donuts on the campsites at San Juan County Park. The last four digits of the license plate were 5824."

He raised an eyebrow. "And you know this how?"

"It was in the papers." She nodded at the window overlooking the small parking lot. "You'll never believe the license plate on the car those kids were driving."

"A red car with damage to the bumper and a plate with the last four digits being 5284?"

"5824," she corrected. "There was no damage to the bumper, but the color was slightly different than the rest of the car, which could mean nothing. But I've got a feeling it does mean something."

He sat back, mouth dropped open. "Did you call the police on those kids?"

A grin spread on her face. "Just Chief Hank. He's a friend of Granny's. He'll probably pull them over and give them a stern talking-to. Scare the daylights out of them." She laughed. "I'll call it even."

Even.

Joey had some things he'd like to erase from his record like that. "It's impressive you remembered the license plate."

"I have a good memory." She shrugged. "Let me know if you have any questions about the menu. I'll be back in a minute."

She glided back through the swinging door as he sat, staring. The tearoom smelled of bergamot and vanilla. The menu was thick, each page a wall of text about the qualities of the tea listed.

He forced his eyes onto the page. *Hot Cinnamon Spice, Harney and Sons – black tea, orange peel, cinnamon, cloves.*

"Ready to order?"

He startled. Eliza was hovering just above him. "Uh, sure. I'll have a pot of this."

"The hot cinnamon spice? That is one of my absolute favorite teas. It's super sweet but doesn't have any sugar."

"How's that possible?"

She looked him dead in the eyes, her eyes round, her lips flat. "It's magic. Tea is magic."

He cracked a smile. "You're funny, you know that?"

"That's what we offer here. Five-star jokes, all day long." She tilted her head. "Anything else for you?"

"Yeah." He leaned forward, his hands resting on the table. "I want you to help me with something."

Eliza tucked the menu under her arm. "Okay."

"Help me find the bank robber."

She raised an eyebrow. "How about I get your tea and—"

"I'm serious. Did you hear about the reward?"

She shook her head.

He went on. "One hundred thousand dollars to whoever can help catch him. We could split it."

"I think you're confused about my skill set," she said. "I make tea. And cupcakes. Do you want a cupcake?"

That had to be the vanilla he'd smelled. Of course he wanted one, but... "This guy has robbed thirteen banks and they can't catch him. You're the only one who talked to him. You must remember something about him with that great memory of yours."

She sighed. "I don't know."

"You *just* solved that vandalism case," he added. "Listen, I've got a plane."

"How's that going to help?" She drew her eyebrows together, her eyes focused.

"I don't know. We can fly around looking for him?"

He stared at her, unblinking. *Say yes. I need you to say yes.*

She stared back at him, took a deep breath, and said, "I'm going to get your tea."

She disappeared again, and this time, Joey could swear he saw her smiling as she turned the corner.

Four

It always came back to the robbery. The robbery, the bank, money, money, money – it was all Eliza could think about. She didn't want to talk about it, too.

Back in the kitchen, her lemon-blueberry cupcakes were cool enough to frost. It was her fifth batch this week, and she'd finally achieved the golden-brown shade Granny's were known for.

Eliza spent hours obsessing over recipes, reading how temperatures of butter or milk affected a bake, tweaking here and there, trying to make them absolutely perfect.

Cupcakes were pleasant to obsess over. Much more pleasant than her mortifying, world-famous trip to the bank two weeks prior.

Eliza knew she'd messed up. She'd helped a guy rob a bank. She'd carried his bags. She had dumped *a bomb* onto the ground!

The ATF determined it was a fake bomb after the fact, but still. She'd done it.

It was so bad, the ATF agent who interviewed her found it hard to believe she wasn't involved with the robbery.

"Are we really supposed to believe you're *that* stupid?" the agent had asked.

Eliza didn't know how to answer that, so she said, "Yes."

The agent had thought Eliza was being sarcastic, but nothing could be further from the truth. They eventually let her leave, but that question echoed in her mind day and night.

She picked up a teapot and added three teaspoons of loose tea, stooping to breathe in the cinnamon before pouring in the boiling water.

It was a lovely tea. She'd already had two cups that morning, but one more wouldn't hurt. She loaded her serving tray, adding two lemon blueberry cupcakes.

"All right, one hot cinnamon spice and one cupcake." She set the teapot and plate in front of him.

Joey peered up at her. "I didn't know it came with a cupcake."

"It's on the house. One of my new creations."

"Are you going to join me?" He nodded toward the second cupcake. "To discuss our reward?"

Eliza scoffed. "I can't help you, but I wish you the best of luck in finding the guy."

He picked up the cupcake and bit into the top, icing dotting his nose. "Wow."

"That bad, huh?" Eliza put her hands on her hips and sighed. "I never promised they'd be as good as my Granny's."

"No, it's not bad. It's *incredible*. This is literally the best cupcake I've ever had."

"You must not eat a lot of cupcakes," Eliza said.

"I eat them *all* the time. I had the alleged best cupcake in the US, and yours blows it out of the water." He took another bite and, with his mouth full, asked, "Can I get three more?"

Eliza laughed. "Sure."

She popped into the kitchen, grabbing a plate of cupcakes and her cup of tea.

"I haven't tried these yet," she said, sitting down across from him. "They need tea to be properly enjoyed."

"Agreed," he said, promptly picking up the teapot to fill his cup.

Eliza used a fork to sample the edge of the cupcake. The blueberry mixture was sweeter this time – she'd added a little extra sugar and vanilla – and the lemon wasn't as overpowering as the last batch, where she'd somehow used the sourest lemons on planet earth.

"Better," she said slowly, "but I think I need to add more vanilla."

He stared at her, wiping a crumb from the corner of his mouth. "How long have you been doing this?"

"Baking cupcakes?" She shrugged. "Since I became the laughingstock of the island."

"Wait, really? You're not a professional?"

She took a sip of tea and shook her head. It was so hot it burned the roof of her mouth – but still so good. "No. I'm just helping here for a while."

He stuffed the rest of the cupcake into his mouth, then added another to his plate. "Too bad. I was going to say you could take your half of the reward money and open a bakery."

Eliza rolled her eyes. "Right. The reward money we'd totally get because we'd find this guy."

"We would. I believe in us."

She couldn't help but laugh – really laugh – this time. "You must be desperate for money."

"Who doesn't need money?" He finished the second cupcake and took a swig of tea. "I'm just saying we would make a unique team."

"Uh huh."

He flashed a smile. His teeth were exceptionally straight – the kind of straight that could only be achieved with braces. Had his parents really needed to do that? Make him more handsome through orthodontics?

"Okay, I know I don't seem super impressive, and you could probably recruit a much more qualified team, but hear me out."

She sat back, tea in hand. She didn't know what he was going on about – recruiting a team – but she liked to watch him talk. His eyes lit up every time she brushed him off, and he had a dimple in his right cheek when he smiled.

"I've worked on a fishing boat in Alaska. I flew a private jet for a billionaire who referred to me as his 'air horse.'"

She frowned. "Weird."

"It was." Joey nodded and went on. "I got shot at flying out of Ghana, and I've flown through thunderstorms and landed in hailstorms. I've survived flying through fog thick enough to send a bomber into the Empire State Building."

Eliza gasped. "You can't joke about plane crashes! Didn't that actually happen?"

A smirk crossed his face, the dimple engaging. "That crash was like eighty years ago. What about the Hindenburg? Too soon to joke about that, too?"

"I don't know." Eliza set her tea down. "Probably."

"Well, sorry." He cleared his throat. "I'm telling you, I'd be a great partner for this."

Men and their confidence. Eliza leaned in. "Let me tell you something. I'm not doubting you. I'm telling you *I'd* be a terrible partner. I ruin everything I touch. I destroy lives – usually just my own, but I'm pretty sure I have the capacity to ruin others' if I put my mind to it."

He narrowed his eyes. "I don't believe any of that."

"Well, it's true." She sat back, arms crossed over her chest.

He downed the rest of his tea and set the cup onto the saucer with a clatter. "I guess I have to prove you wrong. No one who makes cupcakes like that can destroy lives."

Eliza stood. "I assure you I can."

He stood and stepped closer, towering above her. "Will you be here Saturday?"

Her heart leapt a little in her chest. "Why?"

"That's when we start our search. I'll see you then." He smiled, picked up his coat, and walked out.

Eliza was left sitting there, her mouth hanging open as Granny came through the front door.

"Who was that?" she asked, a smile on her lips.

"A man with entirely too much confidence," Eliza said, standing and picking up the plates.

Five

"Do you have five dollars?"

Sheila startled as Patty walked through the back door. "I don't think I have any cash. Why?"

Patty pulled off her coat and scowled. "I owe Joey five dollars. I already gave him twenty, but technically I offered him twenty-five."

"For what? Flying you somewhere?"

Patty looked at Sheila like she had two heads. "Where do you think I need to go? The mental hospital?"

"I don't know. You're the one begging for five dollars!"

Patty turned the water kettle on. "I asked him for a favor with Eliza."

Oh dear. Sheila stood from the table. "I didn't think Eliza had met Joey."

"She hadn't, which is why it was perfect," Patty said with a nod.

"Patty," Sheila said slowly, "you know how hard it's been for Eliza. She doesn't need any –"

"I was *helping* her," Patty hissed, spinning around with a box of tea in her hand. "Do you want a cup?"

"Yes, but –"

Patty cut her off. "There was a table of boys trying to harass her, and I don't know how he did it, but he chased them off."

Sheila shut her eyes and groaned. "She asked us not to get involved!"

"What good was that doing? She's stopped eating, the bags under her eyes look like they belong to the mother of a newborn, and she spends all her free time hiding away in her room."

Sheila took a deep breath. There was no need to argue with Patty. They were on the same side, Eliza's side, and both helpless to get her out of this slump.

The entire thing was ridiculous. It wasn't Eliza's fault she'd walked into the middle of a robbery.

People could be so cruel.

She yanked two teacups out of the cupboard and plopped them onto the counter. "I'm well aware, Patty. Believe me. I don't think of much else."

Before the bank robbery, Eliza had been thriving and Sheila was thrilled. It seemed like her sweet, sensitive daughter had finally found something that worked for her, and it was right here on the island.

Selfishly, Sheila liked having Eliza living with them at the cottage. For so many years, she'd had to fret about Eliza from afar. After she left school, she only grew quieter. More closed off. Alone.

Now, she'd come back to life, reviving Patty's tea shop and running it like a professional. She was home every night, and they got to spend so much time together – eating dinner, watching movies, baking. They even went kayaking once, and even though they didn't make it far, it was wonderful.

Why did she have to be at the bank on that awful day?

"People are acting like that bank robbery was Eliza's fault," Sheila said, shaking her head. "A man stopped me in the grocery store today to tell me Eliza would've thwarted the robbery if I'd raised her with any common sense."

"*Who said that!*" Patty boomed, slamming the box of tea down onto the counter and sending her Golden Retriever, Derby, running under the kitchen table.

Sheila knelt down. "It's okay, Derby. Some people just don't have manners."

"You tell me who it was and I will teach *him* some manners!"

Derby wagged his tail and placed a paw on Sheila's knee. She stroked it with her hand.

"I don't know who it was," she said over her shoulder. "Besides, we're not going to show up at his house to teach him a lesson."

"Speak for yourself," Patty snapped. "When I find out who he was, I'll make sure he will never set foot on this property. I'll have Reggie –"

"You will not have Reggie do anything."

The front door opened and Sheila stopped talking. She mimed zipping her lips and pointed at Patty.

Patty mimicked her, pointing back forcefully.

"Is anyone home?"

Sheila yelled, "We're in the kitchen!"

Eliza walked in, dropping her coat on a chair. Her cheeks were flushed red, her hair wind-blown. "Were you yelling at each other?"

Sheila and Patty looked at one another and said *no* at the same time.

"Hm." Eliza stared at them. "I thought I heard yelling."

"Your mom was just telling me about the permits with the sea pen," Patty said, turning around to pour water for the tea.

Eliza groaned and took a seat at the kitchen table. "I thought that was sorted out?"

Sheila wasn't the best at lying to her children on the fly, but she managed to say, "It is now. It's nothing to worry about. Did you go for a walk?"

"I did." She smiled. "When are they supposed to actually start building the sea pen?"

"That's still up in the air. We have the funding, but—"

"You do?" Eliza's mouth popped open. "When did this happen? I thought you were still waiting for the money from Russell's next movie."

Sheila smiled. What a wild ride this was turning out to be. The initial plan to raise funding was for Russell to do another movie. He hardly wanted to, but his fans were thrilled. He ran a poll on his website, agreeing to do whatever type of movie they picked. All the profits would go to building the sea pen and the surrounding research site for Lottie.

He was now in preproduction for a historical vampire romance with the working title "Fangs of Waterloo," where he played the dashing vampire who risked life and reputation to save a damsel in distress during the famous battle.

Sheila swooned just thinking of him in a waistcoat. "We thought we'd have to wait for the money, but a few of Russell's celebrity friends – actors, directors, even a few musicians – have made some big donations. It's fully funded."

"That's incredible!" Eliza said.

"I just don't believe he can't get Idris Elba out here," Patty said with a sigh. "They have to know each other."

Sheila had to force herself not to smile. "I've told you Russell knows him a little, and while he's a very nice guy, Russell doesn't feel comfortable asking him to—"

"Of course he's a nice guy!" Patty shouted. "I'm sure if Russell sent him a letter with an invitation to see the sea pen, he would at least respond. The worst he can do is say no."

Eliza met Sheila's eyes across the table, then they looked away, suppressing laughter. Patty had been campaigning for her celebrity crush – whom she flatly refused to acknowledge as a crush – to come out to Hollywood's favorite future sea pen for months.

"That's so exciting, Mom. I can't believe this is really happening."

"You and me both." Sheila shook her head.

"Oh!" Patty came to the table with her cup of tea. "Tell her about Russell and the song."

Eliza cocked her head to the side. "What song?"

Sheila didn't need to talk about this right now, but it was the first time Eliza had wanted to talk about anything in weeks.

She clasped her hands together. "Russell wants me to write a song for the movie. But I can't. It feels wrong."

"What? You *have* to! That'd be so cool."

Sheila shook her head. "No, it'd be nepotism, and that would be wrong. It's not like they would put the song in the movie because it's good. They'd only include it because I'm Russell's girlfriend."

Patty let out a cackling laugh. "If not for nepotism, nobody would do anything! It's always what you know." She paused. "No, wait. I meant it's *who* you know. That's what I wanted to say. *Who* you know, and you know Russell. You know who he knows?"

"Idris Elba," Sheila said in a flat tone.

"That's right." Patty nodded, then paused. "Wait, no. Stop teasing me. It's *who* you know. Do you remember how I ended up here? I happened to befriend the guy who owned it, and he agreed to sell it at a deal. That's what's important, you know. Friends."

"Very inspiring story, Patty," Sheila said, and the three of them burst into laughter.

Derby, out of his hiding spot, jumped and put his paws on Eliza's lap, tail wagging, as if he were in on the joke.

Once they recovered, Sheila turned to Eliza. "How are you doing, sweetie?"

Eliza shrugged. "Not bad."

"The cupcakes you made were excellent," Patty said. "Better than mine, I would say."

"No." Eliza smiled. "Though I guess they were pretty good."

Patty went on. "Russell tells me you and Joey are planning to spend some time together this weekend."

"Russell told you that? What a gossip," Eliza said, but she was still smiling.

Patty was about to say something, but Sheila cut her off. "That's nice! It's good for you to have friends here who are under the age of fifty."

"Yes." Eliza laughed. "I love you all, but you do go to bed really early. Actually, speaking of friends, Cora was just telling me she wanted to come and visit soon. Would that be okay, Granny?"

"My home is your home," she said. She took a sip of tea and cleared her throat. "But that girl did steal a lot of money from you, and I will never forgive her."

Eliza snorted into her teacup. "I know. She's not perfect, but she's still my best friend."

Sheila shot Patty a look. "None of us are perfect, are we, Patty?"

Patty pursed her lips. "No, none of you are, except me, but that's taken *years*."

They laughed, Eliza the hardest, and Sheila stood to make some finger sandwiches.

She might not agree with how Patty had handled the Joey situation, but it was the first time she'd heard Eliza laugh in two weeks, so she'd take it.

Six

What were the chances Joey was playing a prank on her? Eliza couldn't stop thinking about it.

It'd be like one of those 90s teen movies her mom had made her watch. Joey was the handsome, popular guy and Eliza was the nerd he'd made a bet to woo. He'd let her hair down and whip off her glasses and suddenly, the rest of the world would be blown away by her inside-out stunning beauty.

There were a few problems with this theory. First, Eliza put her hair down all the time, even while simultaneously taking off her glasses, and no one had ever stopped her in the street to sign her for a modeling contract.

She was no beauty. That much was true, but it didn't bother her. Elizabeth Bennet was always second to her sister in beauty, and it didn't matter. She had her books and her wit – and she'd ended up with Mr. Darcy!

Not that Eliza thought of herself as Elizabeth Bennet. She wouldn't dare to. As much as she loved *Pride and Prejudice,* and as close as their last name Dennet was to Bennet, they were short one sister, and every conversation ended with the girls arguing over who had to be Mary.

Eliza wouldn't admit it out loud, but she knew she was the Mary. Studious but tedious, aspirational but too plain and awkward to be effective.

It didn't matter how hunky Joey was – and he was plenty hunky – he couldn't turn a Mary into anything but a slightly spruced-up Mary.

That was the second problem with the 90s prank theory. Why would someone place a bet on a boring Mary? And why would Joey agree to take the bet?

Eliza kept her head down for the rest of the week, making tea, baking scones, and avoiding indulging in any grandiose thinking.

Then the entirety of Saturday came and went without any sign of him.

As she got ready to close the shop, Eliza realized he had probably been messing with her from the start.

Then, ten minutes before closing time, the front door bell jingled.

"Got any leftover cupcakes you were planning to throw away? Because I'd be happy to take them off your hands."

Eliza peeked up from behind the cash register. He stood there, hands in his coat pocket, grinning at her.

She stood, smoothing her apron. "I usually take our leftovers to the food bank, but if you'd like to steal a cupcake from a baby, sure, I can grab you one."

He paused, then flashed a smile, dimple engaged. "Yeah, forget those kids. Hand over the cupcakes."

Eliza laughed and he rushed to add, "I'm just kidding. Please don't give me one. I wasn't aware of that and now I'll probably never eat one again."

"What about something else? I made a batch of ham and cheese scones that aren't up to par. You could have them."

"Now there's a deal." He stuck out his hand, palm up. "Scone, please."

Eliza smiled and waved for him to follow, leading him into the kitchen and pointing at the plate of misshapen scones. The edges of each scone were lined with char. "Have at it. Sorry they're terrible."

Without a word, he stuffed half a scone into his mouth. "This is so good."

She shook her head. "It's burnt."

"Is it?" Joey chewed slowly. "Nah. It's good."

She rolled her eyes and packed the rejected scones into a bag for him.

He accepted it. "Thank you. Are you in a hurry? I'm sorry I'm here so late. I had lots of flights today, but I was hoping we could still sit down and talk out a plan."

"I never agreed to be part of your scheme."

"You're here, though, aren't you? Waiting to get the rest of my pitch?"

"I work here." She crossed her arms. Hopefully her ears weren't glowing red, betraying her. "I wasn't waiting for you."

"Aw, man. You're not even a little bit curious?" He frowned. "You're putting me out here. I was really hoping to get that money so I could buy my own plane."

Eliza turned, picking up the tea kettle and hiding a smile. "Do you want some tea?"

"I don't want to make you work off the clock."

"Tea is never work." She pulled the lid off of a tea tin. "Another pot of the hot cinnamon spice?"

"Yes, please!"

She made up a teapot and gathered a pair of her favorite cups.

"I can carry that," Joey offered, then added, "Whoa, these are nice."

"Thanks. They're Granny's, for personal use only. She got them when she was living in Japan."

"When did she live in Japan?"

Eliza led the way to a table and Joey followed, carrying the teacups. "She lived all over the place growing up. Her dad was in the army."

"Have you been?"

She took a seat and looked up at him. "To Japan? No. Have you?"

He nodded. "I worked in a factory in Tokyo for six months."

"What? When?"

"When I was young and dumb." He smiled and rolled his eyes. "I wanted to see Japan and I thought I could get hired as a pilot. Turns out it's not that easy, so I ended up at the factory."

"Did you like it?"

"It was awesome. Japan, I mean. The factory, not so much, but I got to travel a lot. Osaka, Sapporo, Niigata, Kyoto – there's so much to see."

"But you didn't stay."

"I missed flying." He shrugged. "Missed it so much I took a sketchy job in Ghana."

She raised her eyebrows. "Oh, right. You mentioned that."

"Yeah. I played pilot for this guy who ran a bunch of cocoa farms. I'm not a hundred percent sure he wasn't a criminal. He seemed to like bribing people."

Eliza poured tea into his cup, then her own. "You've led a more exciting life than I have."

"I just get a lot of bad ideas. The worst ideas, actually."

"Like trying to catch a bank robber."

Joey squinted at her, a smile on his lips. "That's not one of them."

"Luckily, we aren't going to find him." Eliza took a sip, the cinnamon filling her cheeks, then held the cup in front of her. The cup and saucer were tiffany blue with tiny pink roses bursting from the handle and inside the rim.

"We're going to," he said. "I believe in us."

She stared at him. He seemed, at least, to be sincere.

Why wouldn't he be? While he was off exploring the world, she'd been locked in her bedroom, going over all the things she should be doing but was completely unable to do, trapped in a cycle of doubt and anxiety, dipped in self-hatred.

It wasn't even like she'd failed at one thing. That wouldn't have been so bad. Lots of people failed at something.

But Eliza had failed in a much bigger way. She'd failed to become *anything*. All these years, all this promise, and she was nothing. No one.

Steam rose from the teacup sitting in front of him. He met her gaze and kept it.

He was better off searching for the bank robber on his own, and she might've told him that if she didn't find it so hard to look away from that smile of his...

"Where would you start?" she asked.

He took a deep breath and pulled out a pen and a notebook. "Okay, so first, tell me everything you remember about the robbery. No detail is too small."

"Are you sure? The ATF agent got annoyed with me when she asked for my story."

"Why?"

Eliza sighed and set her teacup down. "When she interviewed me, all she said was, 'Tell me about your day.' I said, 'My day?' And she said 'yeah.' So I did, starting from when my alarm went off, how I brushed my teeth and skipped breakfast, how I rushed to the bank, and how I thought about stopping at the coffee shop but I didn't –"

Joey laughed. "She thought you were stalling? Or obfuscating somehow?"

Was that even a word? Eliza had never heard it said out loud, so she said, "I guess."

"I mean it." He stared at her, a pen poised in his hand. "No detail is too small."

She had to look away from him. That dimple. That stare. He was too much. "I'll start with getting to the bank. I pulled into the parking lot and noticed the pickup truck right away, because it was parked on the sidewalk blocking the ATM."

He nodded, writing on his notepad.

"It was a white Toyota Tacoma, at least ten years old, with Goodyear tires. The license plate started with MAC, I don't remember the numbers, though."

"M-A-C," he repeated.

"The back was loaded with stuff and a cover was partially pulled away. The robber was pulling things out. I heard him grunting and came over to help."

"Was he in the wheelchair at this point?"

"Yeah. I know it was dumb to not think how odd it was for someone to drive a truck, get out, and get into a wheelchair." She stole a glance at him. It was one of the many things she'd been ridiculed for online – not recognizing that the robber didn't need a wheelchair.

"He might've just needed it for mobility," Joey said. "Don't let people's comments get to you. They weren't there."

She breathed, releasing the tension in her shoulders. "That's true." Eliza leaned in, her speech picking up speed. "The wheelchair was that blue pleather material, like the kind you see in hospitals. There were stickers on the back, and I was staring at them before he turned around. One was for Harbor Coffee – they're in town. Another was a sticker from Olympia National Park. There were two stickers from Orcas Island, and one from this souvenir shop in town called Whale Gifts. The left armrest of the wheelchair was broken, but the right handle was normal."

Joey furiously scribbled everything she'd said, drawing a big star next to the word wheelchair.

Eliza waited for him to stop writing before continuing. "The guy had a brown wool cowboy hat with a pink-and-gold band around it, and a tassel with gold thread at the end. I thought it looked like a lady's hat. A little small on him, too. Most of his face was covered by a blue surgical mask, but his beard was sticking out from underneath." She paused. "Thinking about it, it was probably a fake beard, because it was really dark and a different color than his hair, and the texture was just weird. Stiff. Plastic-y."

"Interesting."

"There was a tuft of his hair sticking out from the hat. That was a light brown, kind of like your hair, but the beard was black." She thought for a moment. "Yeah, the beard was fake. He had pretty eyes. It was sunny, and I could really see them – dark green, with flecks of brown and blue, with gold around the pupil. His skin was pale, kind of like mine, but with a cooler tone than mine."

"Cooler tone," he mumbled, then looked up. "How old was he?"

"It's hard to say. I would guess anywhere from thirty to fifty."

Joey nodded, adding this to a page titled "Suspect."

"He was wearing a black leather jacket, really loose, with a red-trimmed zipper and golden buttons. He had blue jeans –

Levi's. I saw them when he stood up. He didn't have a wallet in his back pocket or anything. Oh – I guess you can see what he was wearing in the video."

"It's still good to know."

"The jacket was too big for him. It made him look over-weight, but I don't think he is overweight. When he stood up, he was tall – definitely taller than me, about your height."

Joey leaned back and looked at her. "Wow. You remember a lot of detail about this guy. Do you have a photographic memory or something?"

Eliza shook her head. "Not exactly. There's no such thing as a photographic memory. I have a good memory, but..."

She stopped herself. There was no need for him to know about her boring self. Before she'd realized how good her memory was, she thought she was smart. Then she'd gotten to college and met actual smart people.

That was the story of her life. The shame of being smart, but never smart enough.

"This is amazing." Joey scanned the page before flipping to a blank one. "Is there anything else you remember?"

Eliza described his cowboy boots and the curve of his nose. She talked about his coat, the smell coming off him – mint gum and cheap aftershave. She described everything he was wearing down to the mud on his left boot.

"What did he sound like when he was talking to you?" Joey asked.

"His voice was raspy, like he was lowering it or something. I felt like I was talking to the Batman."

Joey burst into a laugh. "Yeah, sounds like Bruce Wayne."

Eliza laughed too, but stopped herself. "He wasn't Batman, though. And I helped him rob a bank."

He stopped writing and looked up at her. "How were you supposed to know he was going to rob the bank?"

"Oh, I don't know, maybe because he insisted on coming in with two bank-robbing bags?" Eliza put her hands over her face and groaned. "It's so embarrassing I didn't catch onto any of it – the beard, the voice, the bags – as being suspicious."

"No, it isn't," he said firmly. "You thought you were helping a man in a wheelchair have an easier day at the bank. You didn't question him because you're a nice person. That's nothing to be embarrassed about."

He seemed to believe that. Eliza picked up her teacup and sat back. "Then we went into the bank and the rest is history."

Joey held the pen at the corner of his mouth, scrawled something, then tapped it on the desk. "I think we have a good start. Lots of details. There's an answer here. I can feel it."

That was kind of him. When she'd told this story before, the ATF agent had told her to "stop trying to come up with a list of useless details."

She cleared her throat. "I'm glad you're optimistic, because I'm not."

"I'm always optimistic." He flipped through the pages. "How about we figure out where he got that wheelchair? It seems like it was local, don't you think? With all those stickers?"

She leaned in. "Huh. Yeah, you're probably right. I don't know why I didn't think of that."

"You're too busy memorizing every single detail around you all the time. It's amazing."

"Thanks," she said sheepishly. It had been a long time since her power of observation was actually useful.

If this could be considered useful.

"Are you ready?" he asked, standing from the table. "We're going to change your life, Eliza."

She looked around. There wasn't anything else to clean, and she didn't have any other plans. "Sure. Why not."

Seven

He couldn't believe his pitch had worked. She didn't seem entirely sold on his idea, but it was better than nothing. She closed the tea shop and Joey offered to drive.

"What'd you say you went to school for?" he asked as they rode into town.

"I went to school with a mission to embarrass everyone."

He burst out laughing. "What?"

She looked at him out of the corner of her eye, a smile on her face. "It's true. I thought it would be fun to get a scholarship and then drop out. I wanted to teach those smug scholarship people a lesson."

He shot her a look. "I bet you had a 4.0."

"No." She turned to look out the window. "3.9."

Joey pulled his eyes away from her and back onto the road ahead of them. "Why did you drop out?"

"I already told you. I didn't like all those people believing in me. I needed to take them down a notch."

He smiled. She was joking, but not exactly. There was some truth to it. He'd get the whole truth out of her eventually. People loved confessing things to him. He had one of those faces – or maybe, being a pilot, they figured they'd never see him again and they could use him as a free therapist.

He preferred it that way. No need to stick around, waiting for awkward silences.

Not that there were any of those with Eliza yet. She deflected everything with jokes. Funny jokes, too, which made it hard for him to keep his footing.

"You're going to go back, then? I mean once we get the reward money."

"Yes. Once we get the reward money, I'll go back." A smile spread across her face. "So, never."

He laughed again. "It's my mission to get you back to school."

"I thought your mission was to buy a plane so you could run your own shady cocoa bean business?"

"Maybe I want to open a scholarship for your education. You can apply by telling me what I was wearing when we met."

She was quiet for a moment, then said, "A black LL Bean bomber jacket, Ray-Ban aviators with golden tint, a gray shirt, dark jeans, and white Nike sneakers with a red swoosh."

He sputtered out a laugh. "Are you kidding me?"

Eliza turned to him, grinning. "Am I right?"

"I don't know!" He pulled into a parking spot in front of Harbor Coffee and stopped the car. "But probably. You're unbelievable."

She bounced her shoulders in a peppy shrug. "Thanks!"

"What were you studying? Becoming a true detective?"

"Physics."

"Physics," he repeated slowly. "I don't think I'm smart enough to be talking to you."

"You don't think you're smart enough to be talking to a college dropout?"

He stared at her, taking in her smile and the glint in her eye. "You know, you don't have to talk about yourself that way."

She crossed her arms over her chest. "What way?"

"Like you're nothing more than your mistakes."

She opened her mouth, but nothing came out.

He spoke again. "For example, you're an expert in memorizing outfits."

"Right." She smiled. "So you're saying I should lean into that?"

"Yeah." He paused. "You know, you remind me of someone."

"A famous designer you flew to a runway show in Milan?"

He laughed. "No. My best friend. Always making jokes at his own expense."

"He sounds great," she said, opening her car door. "Much more fun than a tea shop fashion designer."

She walked ahead of him and opened the door to Harbor Coffee. It looked like they were closing up, but the barista's eyes brightened when he saw her.

"Hey, Eliza!"

"Hey, how's it going?" she asked.

"Not too bad. How are things up in tea city?"

"You know, starting to pick up a little."

He threw a rag over his shoulder. "That's good. Same here. We're starting to get more visitors. More tourists."

Joey walked in behind her. "Hey, do you have any idea where we could find a wheelchair?"

The barista looked up, thinking. "You might be able to borrow one from the senior center. Or I think Grace at Whale Gifts has one she loans out. Do you want me to call and ask her?"

Small towns. Everyone knowing everyone. Joey found it weird. Wasn't it better to be anonymous, to take what you need and get out? Who had the energy to build these relationships?

"No, it's okay," Eliza said. "We'll swing by."

The guy leaned in. "I didn't get to tell you. I stopped by the tea shop last weekend and I tried those new apple crumble miniature pies." He closed his eyes. "They're *incredible.* "

Eliza smiled a shy smile. "Thank you. That was one of my new creations. It's simple, really. Just add more butter than any person should ever consume, then double it."

He laughed. "Butter: the secret ingredient."

"Always."

Joey's eyes darted between them. "Well, thanks for your help. Eliza?"

She nodded. "We'll see you around."

They stepped outside and Eliza pointed down the hill. "The gift shop is down there. You can't just go around asking people about wheelchairs, you know."

"Why not?" Joey shrugged. "I need to borrow one. For my broken-legged relative."

She shot him a side-eye glance. "Is that the story you're going with? I've never heard a bigger lie than when referring to a nondescript 'relative.'"

"Fine. My mom? She broke her leg. How about that?"

"Fractured her femur skiing," Eliza said. "If you make it specific and horrible, people are less likely to question it."

The image of a broken femur popped into his mind and he winced. "Where did you learn that trick?"

"Freshman poetry class. The professor made us write two truths and a lie. She was the only one who got away with her lie because she made it so specific and bizarre. It's stuck with me."

"Such a good student," he said, shaking his head. "It's a shame you're stuck here with me when you could be off at university, learning."

She rolled her eyes. "Come on."

The souvenir shop had a small wooden patio overlooking the harbor. An older woman was outside, squinting into the setting sun from behind dark sunglasses.

"Hello!" Eliza called out as they approached.

"Oh, hi there! I didn't see you coming!" The woman laughed. "Is there anything I can help you find?"

Joey studied the woman, trying to memorize her outfit. White sneakers. Blue shirt. Purple pants. Her name tag said Grace.

Check.

He stared at her, trying to find at least one detail Eliza would be impressed with. Her shoelaces were striped. Was that something?

"I'm looking for new tea towels," Eliza said.

"Oh." She turned and pointed to the door. "Those would be inside. I have a few out here, too."

An elbow flew into his side and he snapped out of his study. "And I'm looking to borrow a wheelchair. My mom is coming to visit, but she broke her femur skiing."

"Oh, poor thing."

"I'm working on the island for a bit for Russell Westwood. Do you know him? I'm flying planes out to his whale sanctuary out on Stuart Island."

He could feel Eliza staring at him, but he couldn't stop talking. "My mom loves sightseeing. I can take her up in the plane, but if she wanted to get around town for a few hours, I'd like to have a wheelchair."

Grace raised a hand to her forehead, wiping away beads of sweat. "I've got one right there. It's a little beat up, but it does the job. You're welcome to it."

She nodded to the corner of the porch where a folded-up wheelchair stood, its silver wheels shining in the sunlight.

Duh. How had he missed that? Surely Eliza hadn't.

"That's so nice of you," Eliza said.

Joey was afraid to open his mouth again, so instead he walked toward the wheelchair and, after wrestling with the levers and pulls, got it to open.

He gave it a push and his eyes fell onto the left armrest, the cushion cracked and twisted. He looked up and saw Eliza staring at it.

"Do you have a reservation sheet or something?" Joey asked. "So I can make sure it's available?"

Grace put her hands on her hips and chuckled. "It's not usually in high demand."

"How often do people borrow it?"

The woman shrugged. "Oh, you know, now and then. I usually leave it out here on the deck in case anyone needs to use it. It always turns back up."

Joey gave it a push. "Thanks! Hopefully I can get it when my mom comes."

"When is she coming, dear?"

"Uh. I don't know." He looked at Eliza.

She sucked in a breath. "Two weeks from Tuesday."

"Right." He nodded. "If she didn't keep track, I think my head would fall off."

That wasn't the phrase, was it? Was it if his head wasn't attached to his body? But how would that work?

Eliza picked up a tea towel with an orca floating in the middle. "This is lovely. I'd like to get another if you have one?"

"Oh yes, inside!" Grace led the way and Eliza followed.

Joey stayed outside, once again wrestling with the wheelchair, trying to fold it back up. The stickers were there, too, just as Eliza had described.

She was incredible. Really incredible. Like an encyclopedia of facts and sassy jokes.

He tucked the wheelchair back into the corner as she emerged from the shop.

"We need to talk," she muttered as she passed.

He pushed the wheelchair aside with a clank and went after her. He couldn't wait to hear what she had to say.

Eight

Eliza couldn't get back to the car fast enough, her heart pounding in her chest, her mind whirring and pinging with ideas.

"I think I have something," she said as they shut themselves inside.

"I know!" Joey's eyes were bright, his smile wide. "That was the wheelchair, right? It had all the stickers you told me about."

Eliza frowned and waved a hand. "Yeah, it was, but there are no security cameras over there. Anyone could've taken that wheelchair. It's a dead end."

"Oh." His smile fell.

He had such a cute smile. It was horrible to ruin it.

"But I just remembered something else," she said. "I'm in all of the local Facebook groups – I live for small-town drama."

"Who doesn't?" Joey said, the corner of his mouth curving upward.

Eliza sucked in a breath. *That smirk*. He could totally pull off a leading role in a 90s movie. "Last week, a guy made a post ranting about people parking on his property. He went on and on about how he was going to set their cars on fire and this was their final warning."

Joey's eyebrows went up, his eyes round. "That's a bit dramatic."

It wasn't just his smile, it was his whole face. He could convey so much with just the tilt of his head. He was so *cute...*

Eliza forced herself to look away. "He's convinced some tourists are trying to move in and claim squatter's rights – and I know it sounds weird, but what if it's the truck from the robbery? Who else would just leave their car abandoned like that?"

"Do you know where he lives?"

Eliza nodded. "He's one of Granny's neighbors. He's nice enough, just private. Sometimes angry."

"Angry and a pyromaniac," Joey said with a nod. "If we step on his property, will he come after us with a flamethrower?"

She tapped a finger to her chin. "You never know. We should bring cookies. You know, just in case."

Joey pulled a plastic bag out of his pocket. "I've got scones!"

The absolute joy on his face made her burst with laughter. She bent forward, covering her mouth, her body shaking with giddy excitement. He followed, laughing like a fool.

Was this really happening? Was she really hunting down robbery clues with a handsome, charming, world traveler like Joey?

It took her a moment to recover. She wiped a tear from her eye and said, "Whew, okay. Shall we?"

It felt like it took forever to get to the property, even though it was only a seven-minute drive. They turned off the main road and drove slowly along the makeshift path, the car rocking left and right in the ruts.

A quarter mile into the property, Eliza spotted it.

"There!" She pointed. "I think that's a truck, right?"

"It's definitely some sort of white vehicle." Joey squinted and stopped the car. "Yeah. It is a truck."

Her heart skipped a beat and made her cough.

"Are you all right?" Joey asked.

She took a deep breath. What were the chances the robber was camping out in that truck? Everyone was obsessing over how he'd managed to get away from the island, but what if he'd never left?

And what if he recognized her and came after them? "Uh, yeah. Just scared. Maybe we should go back and call the police."

"Let me creep a little closer. We'll just peek in."

The car lurched forward and Eliza shot him a look. "*Joey!* What if he's in there?"

"What if it's not even his truck?"

It *looked* like his truck. She squinted to make out the license plate. "I'm pretty sure it's his. I'll call the police."

A person stepped in front of their car and Eliza and Joey screamed.

"Reverse! Get out of here!" Eliza yelled.

Joey fumbled with the gear shifter before putting them into neutral and revving the engine.

The woman walked closer, waving her arms. "Hey!"

Eliza glared at him. "I thought you were good under pressure."

"I'm better with planes," he said in a low voice. "It's fine. We'll just say hello and be on our way."

They got closer and Eliza recognized the woman – Stacy, the ATF agent who'd insinuated she was stupid.

Just what she needed.

Eliza slid down in her seat, doing her best to disappear into the floor.

Joey rolled down his window. "Hey there! Didn't expect to see you here."

She scowled at him. "What are you doing?"

He whipped out the bag of scones and held it up. "I was going to drop off some scones for my neighbor."

"Your neighbor?" She crossed her arms. "What neighbor?"

With her heart still thundering away and the car refusing to absorb her, Eliza made a mistake: she coughed.

Stacy leaned down to look at her. "Miss Dennet. Interesting seeing you again."

Eliza leaned forward and meekly waived. "Hi, Agent Stacy. Ned is my Granny's neighbor and she wanted us to bring over some scones and –"

Stacy cut her off. "This is an active crime scene." She paused. "But you already knew that, didn't you?"

Joey said, "No," just as Eliza said, "Oh?"

She stared at the pair of them. "You weren't poking around, were you?"

This time, they both said no.

She nodded, hands on her hips. "Tell me you're not doing something as dumb as trying to get that reward."

Joey and Eliza looked at each other, each trying to master the look of innocence to varying degrees of success.

"The robber is a dangerous man. You're going to get yourselves killed."

"What? Us? No!" Joey said. "We had no idea this was a crime scene. Did you catch him? The bank robber?"

"I don't have time for this," she said with a sigh. "Get out of here."

"Yes, ma'am!" Joey said.

This time, he was able to appropriately put the car in reverse.

"Hang on," Stacy said, leaning into the window. "Leave the scones."

He handed them to her and she waved them off. The car reversed rapidly down the hill.

When they got back to the road, Joey burst into laughter. "Did you see her face? She was so mad!"

Eliza forced herself to sit up. It still felt like her heart was on the floor of the car. "That was the ATF agent who thinks I'm an idiot."

"*Oh*," Joey said with a groan. "That's why she knew your name."

"Yeah."

"I'm sorry, but isn't this amazing?"

She scrunched her forehead. "What? Proving her point that I'm stupid?"

"You're clearly the opposite of stupid. You were right! That *was* his truck. You almost got there before they did."

"Doesn't mean I'm not still an idiot. She's right. We should stop looking for this guy. He could hurt us. He could—"

The car lurched to the side of the road and stopped.

Eliza gripped the handle of the car door, her knuckles white. "What's wrong?"

"Are you serious right now?" Joey stared at her, eyes narrowed.

"Are *you* serious right now? Why are we stopping?"

He sighed and tilted his head. "Are you really going to make me say it?"

She kept her grip strong. "Say what?"

He unbuckled his seat belt and turned to face her. "You are not an idiot, Eliza. In fact, you're frighteningly smart. You scare people. You scare *me*."

The tension dropped from her shoulders and she laughed.

Joey said nothing. His expression softened and his eyes remained fixed on her, taking her in.

Her stomach was off the car floor now, back up in her throat.

"When I told you that you remind me of my best friend," he said. "I meant it. He's the funniest person I've ever met. Hilarious. My face always hurts whenever I hang out with him."

Eliza looked down at her hands. "Sorry about your weak face, Joey."

He laughed and shook his head. "Stop trying to distract me."

"Distract you from what?" she asked, raising her eyebrows in mock alarm. "Clearly, it's not driving. You're terrible at it."

"I'm trying to have a moment with you here and you're roasting me."

"I didn't know we were having a moment. My apologies."

He smiled. "Thank you. Like I was saying. My best friend has the same problem as you."

She couldn't stop herself. "He's a loser?"

"No," Joey said gently. "He's too hard on himself. He thinks he has to be perfect, that anything else is a failure. Anything *human* is a failure."

Eliza was tempted to crack a joke about not being human, but instead she said, "Ah."

"We don't have to keep looking for the robber. That's fine. But you've got to help me out. You've got to believe in yourself *a little*."

This was getting serious. Eliza fidgeted, pushing her hair behind her ear. "Okay, sure. Fine!"

"I'm not trying to yell at you, but come on! You're a step ahead of the federal agents investigating this crime, and that's without any help. Just your own memories and critical thinking. That's incredible."

She glanced at him. "Thanks."

"I've served literally no purpose except to bring the scones, and still, I feel pretty great about my role in the whole thing."

"Well, that was pretty clever."

"Thank you. I agree." Joey sat back. "I'm happy to keep looking for this guy, especially with you as my partner. But you've got to show some faith."

She looked over at him. "In you?"

"No." His stare was unwavering. "In yourself."

She groaned. "Fine."

"Fine?"

"I said fine!" Eliza crossed her arms.

"Cool." He put the car back into drive. "How about we go to a bakery to get some more scones and talk next steps?"

"Sounds good to me," she said, turning to the window to hide her smile.

Nine

Mackenzie stared at the framed picture at her bedside, the one of the family at her college graduation: Emma and Shelby standing back to back like Bond girls, Mom and Dad smiling, as far apart as could be. Mackenzie was in her cap and gown, grinning at the camera, and Eliza was at her side, looking up at her with round eyes and an earnest smile.

Little sisters. They didn't make them all the same. Eliza had always looked up to her, perhaps too much. Eliza's face was the picture of adoration here. Like Mackenzie could do no wrong.

Mackenzie wasn't perfect, though, as the past few weeks had clearly showed.

She heaved herself out of bed. How was this happening? She was supposed to be the one who had it all together. The big sister with all the answers.

She was twenty-seven years old! Too old to throw her life and everything she'd worked for away because of a – what? Because of a boy?

It was too shameful to say out loud, but it was eating her alive. Maybe the one person she could tell was Eliza.

Eliza never judged and she didn't lecture. If anyone would listen, it was her. She might even be able to help.

Mackenzie's phone almost slipped out of her sweaty hand as she hit call.

Eliza picked up after three rings. "Hey!"

"Hey, it's me."

"How are you doing?"

"Good," she lied. "How are you?"

Eliza sighed dramatically. "Oh, you know, just in hiding since becoming internet famous. Or infamous. I'm not sure."

Mackenzie frowned. "Has it been bad? I thought it would've blown over by now."

"Eh, you know. Things linger."

"I'm sorry."

"Don't be! It's okay. What's new with you?"

Mackenzie took in a shaky breath. "Ah, well—"

"Did you and Steve announce your takeover of the company yet?"

She shut her eyes. How arrogant she'd been with Steve, joking how they were the company power couple. How naïve she'd been to trust him at all. "No, but he announced something else."

"Shoot, is he leaving? Did he get another job?"

Her throat was tight. She tried to swallow and ended up coughing. Maybe she wasn't ready to talk about it. "No. Never mind."

"Oh, come on. I'm sorry. I'll stop guessing."

A glass of water sat on the bedside table. She probably hadn't been drinking enough water – not enough to keep up with all the crying. She took a sip. "I was thinking of coming to visit you guys again."

"Really? I would love that! Are you going to bring Steve this time?"

She set the glass down. Why had she called if she wasn't going to talk about it? What was the point in hiding it from Eliza, of all people? "We broke up."

"*What?*"

She cleared her throat. "It's so bad. I can't tell you, Eliza."

"It's okay! You don't have to tell me. I'm so sorry, Mackenzie. I know how much you loved him."

A sob rose from deep inside her chest and rocked her forward. Mackenzie tried to keep her lips pressed tightly shut, but a whine escaped.

"Mack? Are you okay?" The pitch rose in Eliza's voice. "What happened?"

"He's engaged, Eliza." She swallowed back the tears and mucus in her throat. "Steve is engaged."

"How is that possible?" She was yelling now. "He was dating you!"

"He said – well, he announced he was engaged to Addy two weeks ago."

"*What!* After all this time telling you no one at work could know about you guys because it was unprofessional and..." Eliza stopped. "Oh. Was he...?"

Mackenzie got a tissue and blew her nose before speaking again. "Yeah. You figured it out faster than I did. Turns out I was the other woman and I didn't even know it."

"That can't be right."

"It is. I feel crazy. Like I imagined the whole relationship or something. I don't know, Eliza. He said we were always good friends, that we can keep being good friends."

"You didn't imagine it! He came to visit for your birthday, and he got you three dozen roses on Valentine's Day this year. Remember that?"

Her lips were numb from forgetting to breathe. "Oh yeah. I forgot he did that."

"Those weren't 'good friends' roses! What is the matter with him?"

Mackenzie looked down. She wasn't crying because of the humiliation or the shame.

Well, that was part of it, but mostly she was crying because of something far worse.

She missed him.

What was wrong with her?

"I don't know what to do."

Eliza gasped. "He's your manager now, right?"

"Yeah. He got promoted."

"Ew. Wait, is he *her* manager too?"

Mackenzie blew her nose again. "Yeah."

"This is a hostile work environment." Eliza sighed. "I'm so sorry, Mack."

"It's bad, but I can't quit. I've gotten so far and..." Her voice trailed off.

"Don't quit, then. Can you come and visit? The bottom bunk in my room is wide open."

"Our sales numbers are down and I can't take time off."

"Oh, because it'll hurt *his* numbers for *your* numbers to be down?"

"Yes," Mackenzie said weakly.

"Okay, this ends now. You need to get out of there. You're confused and you need a hug. I'll make cupcakes and I'll have Russell send the private jet."

Mackenzie laughed. "Please don't do that."

"Remember when he flew you out for Christmas?"

She smiled. That was a happier time. As dramatic as it sounded, she felt like she'd never feel happy again. "I still dream about the French chocolates the flight attendant gave us."

"Come on, just come out for a few days. Please?"

She hadn't been able to get much done that week, insisting she was sick and working from home.

All she'd done was fall apart, walking from one room to the next. At least if she was with Eliza, she'd have someone to talk to. "Okay, fine. But I'll fly out myself. Don't call Russell."

"Good, because I don't think he has the money for a private jet and Mom would yell at him. Yay! I can't wait to see you! Tell me when you're coming—Granny will make a feast."

It wasn't just Eliza. There was Granny, of course. And Mom. Three whole people who would be happy to see her, who knew she hadn't imagined the whole relationship. "I will."

"Love you!"

Mackenzie smiled. "Love you, too."

Ten

Flying people to and from the sea pen was honest work and Joey wasn't going to complain about it. There was no one shooting at him. He didn't have to wear three layers of pants to keep his blood from freezing in his veins, and not only did Russell pay him well, he also covered fuel for personal use and "training," which was basically Joey flying around for fun.

At the same time, having to wait an entire week before he could take Eliza in the air for her first flight was *killing* him.

While he was busy making chitchat with contractors and veterinarians, Eliza was in the tea shop researching everything she could find about the previous robberies.

She managed to bake something new every day, too – macadamia nut cookies yesterday, birthday cake sugar cookie bars today.

Joey stopped in every day after work for her updates and new recipes. His favorite so far were the Earl Grey sugar cookies, which came on the same day Eliza had a breakthrough on the case.

"He's getting bolder," she said, spreading a stack of papers onto the table in front of him.

"Mm, yes," Joey said, his mouth full of cookies. "Did you dust these with sugar?"

"Yes," she said impatiently. "Look at this. His first robbery, they think, was in Tacoma. He robbed the tellers and only got away with a few thousand. Kept it quick."

He took a sip of tea. "Yeah. Is this cinnamon, too?"

"Can you please focus?"

"Yes, of course. Focused."

"Then he hit the branches in Olympia, Leavenworth, and Portland in the same way. They didn't even realize the Portland one was him until recently. That was where he started to get creative."

"Ah yes, Portland. That's a fun place to land."

She pointed to a red star she'd made on the map. "This was the first time he cleaned out the ATMs, too. That was when he started making more money. A comment from one of the news stories piqued my interest."

"A news story from back when he did it?"

"Yeah. One of the employees they interviewed said the guy had to be a bank employee. He knew too much of the lingo and seemed to know his way around."

Joey shifted in his seat. Now that was interesting. "Why did they decide this robbery was done by the same guy?"

"The pattern, I guess. Hitting all these branches, getting in and out quickly. Working alone."

"Interesting. Is that where we'll start, then? In Portland?"

"I wish we could get an employee list," she said with a groan. "That would make it so much easier."

"I'll just ring up Stacy, our favorite ATF agent, and ask her for a list."

"Better you than me," Eliza said, then paused. "You know, sometimes websites have a directory. You can look at all the employees, maybe even use a function to see previous lists..."

"You're thinking this guy got fired?"

"Fired or laid off, maybe? How bold would you have to be to keep working at the bank you're robbing?"

"He could be one of those shy, introverted bank robbers."

"Yeah, sure." She took a bite of a cookie, chewing slowly. "These are supposed to be softer."

"They're perfect," he said, picking up his third. "And yes, there are shy bank robbers. There was that guy who only handed notes and never spoke during robberies. When he got caught, he said he was funding a charity."

"You believed him?"

Joey frowned. "Don't you?"

She sighed. "I don't trust anyone anymore."

"Not even me?" He regretted saying it as soon as it was out of his mouth.

She grinned. "No, I trust you, Joey. Enough to put my life in your hands when we take to the skies."

The last bite of cookie got caught in his throat. Maybe they were a touch dry. Too much powdered sugar on top.

Or maybe it was time he told her more about his past and what had brought him here.

"Should I not trust you?" she asked.

If she hadn't figured it out by now, what was the point in ruining their fun?

"Ha. No, you should." He forced a smile. "I'm honored."

Eleven

Their plan was to leave at sunrise. Eliza didn't mind the early hour. Her best bakes were usually done at dawn, and she found the solitude comforting.

Today, however, felt different. The quiet left her thoughts in a jumble, looping around robberies, facts about the robber, interviews she'd read, and of course, what she'd said to Joey.

She had the urge to wake Granny just to fill the silence.

That wouldn't help, though. Granny would have questions, and Eliza didn't want to lie, so instead, she washed her face, dabbed on a touch of makeup, and slipped downstairs.

In the kitchen, she debated if her churning stomach could handle breakfast. On the one hand, eating might cause an embarrassing bout of motion sickness on the plane. On the other hand, she'd already fainted at one bank. She wasn't about to do it again.

She settled on a piece of toast and a cup of black tea. It wasn't much, but it was enough. She held the hot mug in her hands and replayed last night's conversation with Joey in her head.

When she'd said she trusted him, it seemed to do something to him. He'd looked down, blushed. Was it bashfulness she'd seen?

Eliza couldn't figure it out. Maybe she'd been too forward? Shown her cards too soon?

But it was true! She was going to get on that plane and trust he wasn't going to fly them into the ground. Eliza wasn't afraid of flying in general, but she'd never known the pilot before. She'd never made a pilot laugh so hard that tea came out of his nose. She'd never heard about a pilot's exploits and bad decisions that spanned the literal world.

She'd never wondered if pilots could hold hands while flying, or if they had to keep both hands on the wheel...

Did planes have steering wheels? She had no idea, and she shouldn't be thinking about trying to hold his hand. Elizabeth Bennet didn't waste her time thinking about holding Mr. Darcy's hand – not until long after his first proposal!

She pulled on her coat and stepped outside. The sun had just begun to rise and a cool, foggy mist drifted from the rocky beach.

Eliza had the brief thought that the fog might ground them, but then she saw Joey coming over the hill and had to remind herself not to gasp. His bomber jacket was open, exposing a white shirt beneath. For a brief moment, he looked just like Mathew McFadyen's Mr. Darcy, coming to propose.

But he isn't coming to propose, she reminded herself. *This isn't a romance. It's a mystery.*

"Hey!" he called out. "Beautiful morning for a flight."

Eliza snapped back to reality. "Is it?"

"Yeah, the fog is pretty minor. Not a concern," he said, reaching her with a wide grin on his face. "Everything is good to go – unless you've changed your mind."

Even his hair looked a little feathered. If she called him Fitzwilliam, would he get the reference?

She really was going mad. "Nope. I'm ready to go and I'm not looking back."

"What about looking down?" he asked.

"I'd like to look down and see the islands from above."

"Good, because I heard a humpback was spotted on the west side, and I thought we could fly over and have a look."

Fly over and have a look. What freedom he had. No wonder he was always so happy. "Sounds good!"

He led the way down the hill to Russell's property. The new dock and seaplane floated in the mist. Joey opened the seaplane's door and offered a hand to help her step on board.

Just like Mr. Darcy helping Elizabeth into the carriage after the ball at Netherfield...

Eliza accepted, stepping onto the plane. Her own hands were freezing, but Joey's were warm and dry.

"Here's your headset," he said, handing her the bulky thing. "Once the engine is on, we'll only be able to hear each other through the headsets. You'll notice a lag between when you start talking and when it picks it up, so keep that in mind."

"Is that why pilots always start with an 'Uhhhh?'"

He sighed. "Uhh, yes, that is correct."

She laughed and put the headset on. "Uh, roger that."

"I'm just going to go through my pre-flight checklist and we'll be on our way."

Eliza nodded, then pretended not to watch him. His focus was entirely on the checklist, which was very annoying, because she would've preferred his attention to be on her.

At the same time, she liked watching him flip switches and push buttons before finally starting the engine.

"Welcome to Joey Airlines," he announced as they floated across the water. "I'll be your pilot today. We've got an exciting trip planned, with our first stop at Lime Kiln State Park for whale watching, then onto Portland, Oregon to investigate a different type of whale."

She turned to him, her eyebrows scrunched. "What?"

"Don't they call big gamblers 'whales'?"

Eliza laughed. "Oh. They do. Is that part of your theory now? That this guy has a gambling problem and he's robbing banks to fuel that?"

"Yes. Based on nothing, that is my theory." He nodded, then turned to her. "Are you ready to be amazed?"

She realized she was gripping her seat tightly with both hands. She let go. "Yes!"

They picked up speed, zipping along the water. Eliza held her breath as the plane popped into the air without any sort of fuss, the shore shrinking beneath them.

She leaned over to look through his window. "I can see my house from here!"

He glanced down at her before pointing. "And there's the tea shop!"

Her excitement made her forget herself. She sat back up. "Very cool."

They flew over San Juan Island, Eliza glued to her window, trying to trace the streets she knew through the sea of green.

"Last report was the whale was surfacing right by the lighthouse," Joey said.

They did several passes but had no luck spotting the whale.

Eliza didn't care. It would've been nice to find a humpback, but seeing the park from this angle was enough of a treat.

She had thought it was stunning from the water that time Mom and Russell had convinced her to go kayaking, but this? It was unreal, the world unfolding beneath them as they glided in the golden sky.

The plane dipped, Eliza's stomach along with it, and she once again clung to the edges of her seat.

"Sorry, I was adjusting," he said. "Nothing to worry about."

"Have you ever crashed before?" she asked, loosening her grip.

He turned to look at her, eyebrows raised. "Do you really want to talk about crashes right now? It's bad luck!"

"I'm sorry!" she put her hands up. "Carry on."

After ten minutes, they gave up on the humpback and flew south toward Portland.

Joey didn't speak again until there was nothing beneath them but a sea of blue. "I did crash once."

She shot him a look. "No, you didn't."

He nodded. "I did. It was early on in my career. I'd just gotten my license."

"What happened?"

He was quiet for a moment. "I made some mistakes."

Oddly vague for him. "Was everyone okay?"

"They all lived, yes."

She crossed her arms over her chest. "You're messing with me."

He looked at her and shook his head. "I'm not."

"Does Russell know?"

"What? No!" Joey laughed. "He didn't ask."

"I'm not going to let you tease me right now."

She turned and looked out of the window. There was a mass of blue beneath them. They were so high; falling would feel endless. Falling and falling and falling, then hitting the water – how deep could she go, plunging to the bottom?

Rationally, she knew crashing anywhere would result in a swift death, but the ocean made it look almost inviting.

Crashing on land might be better, though, because they had a chance at being found. Being out here meant being swallowed by the sea.

"It was just two of us on the plane when I crashed." He glanced at her and added, "No broken bones. Just one broken heart."

A sliver of land appeared ahead of them and Eliza let out a breath. "Uh huh."

"Are you okay over there?"

She spun to look at him. "Yeah. Great. Why do you ask?"

"I'm sorry. I won't talk about crashes. We're not going to crash. I promise."

He placed his hand on top of hers for the briefest of moments and squeezed.

Eliza's breath caught in her throat, but she quickly recovered. "I just miss earth a little bit."

Joey laughed. "We'll be back on earth soon."

. . .

Landing in Portland was a breeze. They walked to the bank, and when Eliza explained who she was, the manager emerged from her office to talk to them.

"I was so sorry to hear about the San Juan branch being robbed," she said, shaking Eliza's hand. "It's such a frightening experience. I didn't sleep for at least a month after our robbery. How are you doing?"

It was the first time Eliza realized what had happened to her was more than just embarrassing – it was traumatic.

Obviously. If it had happened to anyone else, she would've been worried for them. But since it had happened to *her*, she'd only been annoyed with herself and her poor reaction.

They talked to the manager for half an hour, and though the woman was open and friendly, she didn't have any information to share. The only thing Eliza took away from the conversation was that it might be okay to give herself some grace.

They left the bank and stood outside under the gorgeous midday sun.

"I guess we can try Tacoma next," Eliza said.

"Or," Joey said slowly, "we can find a little breakfast place and hang out here for a while."

She made a face at him. "We're on a mission, Joey! We're not here to have fun."

"Aren't we? Isn't that what we're always here for?" He sighed. "Let me buy you a coffee, at least, and we'll see where the day takes us."

Eliza was feeling much hungrier since getting off the plane. She agreed to breakfast, then Joey convinced her to catch a cab to the zoo and, after that, to stroll through Washington Park.

Then he was hungry again, and they were having so much fun, they ended up getting high tea at a fancy hotel downtown.

In the end, they never made it to another bank, but Eliza wasn't too torn up about it. It only meant they'd have to go out again.

Twelve

With a plate of Eliza's rejected danishes in hand, Sheila made the short trek to Russell's house.

"I've got good news," he said as he opened the door.

"Oh?" His bubbly optimism was infectious. Even the stern-faced contractor got giddy after hanging out with Russell. "I doubt you can top what I've got – Eliza's apricot danishes."

He paused, looking down at the offering in her hand. "It's close, but I still can beat it."

Russell kissed her, then took her coat and hung it in the closet. Sheila took a seat at the kitchen island, breathing in the smell of fresh coffee.

As much as she loved living in the cottage with Patty, nothing quite beat Russell's house. It was big, but still cozy. Updated, but not overdone. He kept it so neat, and he always had something to offer – local coffee, freshly baked bread, or extra-sweet fruit he couldn't wait to share.

If she thought too much about it – about *him* – reality unraveled around her, like how saying a word too many times made it seem unreal.

She had a boyfriend and he was *Russell Westwood*. He was gracious, and funny, and distractingly handsome, and, of all things, a famous movie star.

There were still times she'd wake from sleep with a start and it hit her all over again. She was dating *Russell Westwood*. He was a real person. A real-life dream.

He was *hers*.

"Unfortunately, I've got some bad news, too," he said, creases forming at his eyes. "Coffee or tea? I just got a new black pumpkin tea. I've been meaning to give some to Patty."

"I'll stick with coffee for now, thank you." Sheila stood to get plates for the danishes. "I'll take the good news first – pairs better with the sugar."

His face brightened with a smile and she caught herself staring. He'd had to shave his beard for his upcoming movie, and Sheila was still getting used to this new handsome version of him. It made his smiles even more boyish, the mischief always dancing in his eyes.

"I talked to the music supervisor for the movie. She's made all her selections, and guess whose song they picked for the song when the couple breaks up?"

"Regina Spektor?"

"No."

"Brandi Carlile?"

"No, it's not—"

She cut him off with a gasp. "Adele!"

He narrowed his eyes, a playful smile on his lips. "You can't just keep naming people you like."

Sheila took a bite of danish. "No, I can. I could go on for hours."

"Fine, then I'll just tell you. It was you, Sheila Wilde!"

She shut her eyes. "Russell. You can't be excited about this. I didn't earn it."

He took a seat next to her with a mug of tea for himself and one of coffee for her. "I knew you were going to be prickly about it, so I didn't mention who you were when I submitted the song."

"Yeah, right."

"I'm serious. I added your song and a bunch of other ideas for consideration all at once. I didn't say a word. They had no idea who you were, let alone that you're my girlfriend."

Sheila smiled. "But still, you passed it along. That's cheating."

"It isn't, because you could just have easily submitted it yourself, except you kept refusing so I had to do it for you."

He was *technically* right. She hadn't wanted to throw her name in because she thought it was so unlikely they'd pick her. If what he was saying was true...

"Your song is going to be in the movie." He put his arms out for a hug. "*Fangs of Waterloo,* here you come!"

She wasn't going to turn down a hug. She pulled him in and rested her head on his chest. "Yay."

"I'm going to pretend you said that with some enthusiasm." Russell pulled back to look at her. "You'd better get to work on finishing the rest of this album, because people are going to come looking for more Sheila Wilde hits and you need to be ready."

"It'll be done when it's done," she said simply. "I'm not trying to become famous here. You've warned me against that."

"Fine, keep being yourself." He grinned at her. "I'm so proud of you."

Steam rose from the coffee mug and Sheila stared at it. There was a time when she would've given anything for her ex-husband to say even a curt "not bad" about one of her songs.

She'd been through enough therapy to be able to say, without bitterness, that he was too small of a man to let her be anything, win anything, achieve anything.

Russell, on the other hand, not only wanted the world to see her, he wanted to shout her name from the rooftops.

Water pulled to her eyes. Her nose was hot.

"Thank you." She looked up, locking onto his clear blue eyes. "I'm happy about the song."

"But it's not all you'd hoped it would be?"

She smiled and the tears passed. "It's more than I hoped it would be, because you're so happy for me. That's what matters."

Russell sighed and pulled her in for another hug. "I'm fine being happier for you than you are. I'll hold this spot until you're ready for it."

"Perfect." Sheila pecked him on the cheek and picked up her coffee mug. "What's the bad news?"

"It's the sea pen, of course." He picked up a danish and took a bite. "Oh, these are great. Why did she reject them?"

Sheila shrugged. "You know Eliza. The apricots weren't arranged right."

He laughed and took another bite. "We've got a problem with the lodge."

"Ah."

The property Russell and the whale rehabilitation team had secured for the sea pen site was an old fishing lodge. Renovations have been underway to make lodgings for the veterinarian team and staff, and they'd hit problems every step of the way.

"What went wrong now?"

"They found asbestos in the walls. The contractor said we should just tear it down to the studs at this point."

She groaned. "I'm sorry, honey. That's going to take forever, isn't it?"

"Nah, it's okay!" he said brightly "It's a relief in some ways. We were trying hard to retrofit everything, but now I can make sure it's all perfect. They're getting to work right away. I thought we could fly over today and check on the progress."

"That sounds lovely." She paused. "You know, I take back what I said. I love having a personal pilot take us on trips whenever we feel like it."

"Fame and fortune have already gotten to your head," he said, arms crossed over his chest.

Sheila winked at him. "I tried to warn you."

. . .

They walked out to the dock to meet Joey, the calm sea framing their view.

"I offered to pay for fuel so Joey can practice flying or have fun, whatever he wants to do," Russell said.

"That's nice."

"Last weekend, he and Eliza apparently went all the way out to Portland and—"

Sheila cut him off. "Excuse me. What?"

"Did Eliza not tell you about it?"

Her eyes could not get any wider. "No! How could you hide this from me?"

"I didn't hide anything!" He put his hands up. "I thought you knew."

"This is more interesting to me than both the asbestos and the song put together, and you wait until *now* to mention it?"

He cocked his head to the side. "Really?"

"Yes! How can you not realize that my daughter going on a flying date with—" She spotted Joey walking down the hill and dropped her voice to a whisper. "We'll talk about this later."

Russell laughed and covered his mouth. "Sure. Sorry."

Joey said his hellos and promptly got them into the air. Sheila managed to resist asking any probing questions, watching as Joey joked with Russell, laughing and carrying on.

Why hadn't she realized it before? Of course Eliza would like this guy. He was interesting, good-looking, and seemed worldly. Maybe *too* worldly for Eliza?

Sheila sat silently, thinking of what would happen if Joey hurt Eliza. She'd have no choice; she'd have to mount an argument to Russell as to why he had to be fired.

Thankfully, before her imaginary argument reached a crescendo, they landed. Sheila managed a polite smile to Joey before stepping onto the dock.

They didn't spend long at the site. They were still mainly in the demolition phase but making good progress. Russell wanted to get her thoughts on the new plans for a dining hall and a spate of guest cabins. She agreed it looked good, and they were off and back on the plane with Joey.

On the way back, she and Russell discussed Lottie's most recent health report. They, along with the rest of the rehabilitation team, got the reports every month.

Her worries about Lottie taking a turn for the worst at the last moment weren't coming to fruition. Lottie was eating well and gaining weight. Russell had made sure to upgrade her food supply to the best quality fish and, on the recommendation of a new veterinarian, increased the amount she was getting. The trainers had stopped Lottie's performances at the park, now focusing on increasing her strength and stamina.

They'd also introduced Lottie to live fish. So far, Lottie had befriended all the salmon placed in her tank, playfully chasing them and letting them swim in her wake.

She was too adorable. Sheila could hardly stand it, and she never would have imagined the joy she'd feel over reading how many tons of salmon an orca had eaten, or how she'd played peek-a-boo with a fish.

Could life get any stranger, or more beautiful?

Her answer came as they flew back to San Juan Island. Waving at her from the cottage's patio were four women: Eliza, Patty, and what looked like Cora and Mackenzie.

Even though they couldn't see her up in the sky, she grinned and waved back like a fool.

Thirteen

Surprising her mom never got old. This time, Eliza even got to enlist Joey's help to create a dramatic entrance for their surprise guests.

It worked like a charm. Back on land, Mom broke into a run when she spotted them, her arms in the air, waving frantically.

"Girls!" she yelled. "You did it again!"

Eliza laughed and waved back. "Got you!"

Cora's eyes were focused on Russell.

"It's *actually* him," she whispered, grasping Eliza's arm. "He's getting closer. Eliza, he's getting closer!"

She managed to wiggle out of her grip. "Did you think I'd made the whole thing up?"

Cora puffed out her cheeks and let out a measured breath. "I don't know what I thought."

"You look like a puffer fish," Eliza said. "Pull yourself together."

"I didn't know you like, *meant it,* meant it."

Mackenzie shot her a side eye. "That doesn't make any sense."

"Are there movie stars here all the time?" Cora tried fixing her hair, an impossible task against the gusts of wind from the ocean. "Because I think I'm ready to fall in love again."

Mackenzie and Eliza burst into laughter just as their mom reached them, wrapping them both in a hug.

"What's so funny?" Granny asked, then immediately jumped to, "Sheila, do you and Russell want pepperoni rolls?"

"I thought those were all for me," Mackenzie said, looking over her shoulder.

Granny waved a dishtowel in the air. "Don't be greedy. I've got plenty to go around."

"I had no idea you were coming to visit, Mackenzie!" Mom paused, studying her face. "Is everything okay? You look upset."

Mackenzie shot a look at Eliza, who put her hands up. "Hey, I didn't tell her anything."

She turned back to Mom and heaved a sigh. "Everything's fine. Steve and I broke up and I wanted to get away for a bit. Eliza made me come."

"I'm so sorry, sweetheart. Do you want to talk about it?"

She shrugged. "Maybe later."

Russell reached them and Cora stepped forward, sticking out her hand.

"It's nice to meet you. I'm Cora, Eliza's childhood best friend and film enthusiast."

"And fashion icon," Mackenzie added dryly.

"Yes, and fashion icon," Cora said.

Eliza rolled her eyes. "You can ignore her."

He was too polite to do so and accepted her handshake. "Nice to meet you, Cora."

Cora pressed on. "You're very handsome in person, did you know that? Taller than I expected."

"Taller? That's not one I get often."

"Coincidentally," Cora said, leaning closer, "I recently broke up with my boyfriend, too. Do you know anyone single and looking?"

Eliza chortled a laugh. "Cora. Please go sit down."

She raised her chin defiantly. "You have to go after what you want in life. I'm always telling you that, Eliza."

"Yeah, I know. Right now, I want you to stop talking."

A smile broke across Cora's face. "Touché."

Granny herded them onto the patio and they enjoyed an early dinner. Everyone talked all at once, shouting over each other about the tea shop and the sea pen and Cora's new passion for theater.

The one thing they didn't talk about was Steve. Mackenzie didn't bring him up and they knew better than to ask.

After they'd cleared the table, Mom and Russell had to discuss some details with the contractor, so the girls were left outside to themselves.

"What do you do here all day, Eliza?" Cora asked. "It's pretty and all, but it looks super boring."

Eliza shrugged. "I like boring."

"It is so beautiful here." Mackenzie stared out at the horizon, her eyes blocked by oversized black sunglasses.

"Seriously, though." Cora stood and stretched her legs. "Is this whole island like a retirement community?"

Eliza laughed. "No, Cora. Just because there's no nightclub doesn't mean it's a retirement community. I have a couple of friends in town."

Should she mention Joey? It seemed unwise. Best to keep their relationship to herself, away from scrutiny.

That was what she decided, yet in the next moment heard herself say, "I've been hanging out with Russell's pilot, Joey. He's awesome."

"Oh!" Cora's expression brightened. "Is he a pilot to the stars?"

"Sometimes, I guess? He flies the whale researchers and contractors and painters—"

Cora put up a hand. "Ugh, boring."

"If it's so boring here, why did you beg me to bring you along?" Mackenzie asked, arms crossed.

Uh oh.

Mackenzie and Cora clashed on a good day. A visit with both of them being so much themselves could go wrong quickly.

It was Eliza's own fault. She'd wanted to see them. She had been greedy and now she was sitting at the table with a hot frying pan full of oil and a glass of cold water.

"Probably because she's flat broke," Eliza said with a teasing smile. "Be careful she doesn't try to rob you."

Cora covered her face with her hands and laughed. "I'm still sorry I stole our rent money, Eliza. I'm not just broke. I'm in debt! I took out all this money and it's just been so bad."

"I thought you were working for your dad's company?" Eliza asked.

"No, he fired me. Can you believe that?" She paused, a smile dancing on her lips. "I mean, I deserved it, but how *rude*."

Mackenzie turned to her, an astonished smile on her face. "How bad do you have to be at your job for your own father to fire you?"

"Extremely bad," Cora said with complete sincerity.

Mackenzie erupted into laughter. "I like your honesty, at least."

"Anyway, enough about me. How are you doing, Eliza? Are people still bugging you about the robbery?"

She shrugged. "You know, not as much anymore."

"It's horrible, what happened to you." Cora shook her head. "When you think about it, we're so out of control of our lives, aren't we? You went to the bank, a totally innocent move – responsible, even, because that's where normal people get money, not from shady bookies."

Mackenzie took off her sunglasses. Her eyelids were puffy. "You've been going to shady bookies?"

Cora waved a hand. "Just some of those payday lenders. Have you ever had to use one of them?"

Her mouth dropped open. "No!"

Eliza had to bite her lip to keep from laughing. "Cora likes to live on the wild side."

"I'm just a woman who was coddled too much growing up," Cora said, shaking her head. "Now I'm catching up. It's honestly *fascinating*, the things people do."

"I need to hear more. For my mental health," Mackenzie said, leaning in.

An idea kept nagging at the back of Eliza's mind. She had to say something. "Are you really running with a rough crowd?"

"More like running *from* a rough crowd. I owe a lot of people money. I'm definitely going to get a job now, though. No more messing around. I'm waiting to hear back on an interview for a position as a therapist."

"You're going to be a therapist?" Mackenzie shook her head. "I'm sorry, I don't mean to be rude, but—"

"I know, no offense taken. I get it. I'm a screw up, but I'm a self-aware screw up. I have my master's in counseling! Once I get this job, I can pay everyone back."

Normally, Eliza was good at keeping secrets. She knew she shouldn't say anything about Joey, or their search, or their silly plan...

"Would you happen to know anything about the bank robber? Maybe heard whispers about who he was?"

Cora's eyes widened. "Everyone is talking about it! And no, if I found out who'd embarrassed my best friend at the bank, I'd have already turned him in."

She smiled a small smile. "I'm trying to look for him."

"What?" Mackenzie shook her head as if she'd been slapped. "How? Why?"

"There's a reward." She smiled. "And I have a partner."

Mackenzie cocked her head to the side. "You have to tell us."

Maybe she shouldn't tell them. Maybe Mackenzie would scold her, but at the same time...Eliza never had the good story. Her life wasn't the one packed with excitement or new people.

How could she not tell them about someone as cool as Joey?

She smiled. "It's a lot. I'll get some tea."

Fourteen

With the changes at the sea pen site, Joey was in high demand, flying as many workers and supplies as he could fit into the plane.

He didn't mind. He liked being busy and it was his job, after all – but he felt himself pulled to the tea shop. Every time he took off, his mind was back on the ground, wondering what it'd be like to meet Eliza's mysterious older sister and her wild best friend.

When Eliza had first told him they were going to visit, all she would tell him was, "They're both lovely, but very different. It's...complicated."

Joey liked complicated. It gave him something to think about on the long flights between Seattle and Stuart Island while his passengers discussed drywall and ductwork and filtration systems.

It took two days before he snagged himself an invite to the tea shop. Eliza was hosting a board game night for the patrons, and both Mackenzie and Cora had insisted on participating.

"You're lucky," Eliza said when he met her in the tea shop kitchen. "We only had one more spot at our table."

"I know I'm lucky," he said, loading the dishwasher with cups. "This is the social event of the season."

She rolled her eyes. "I wouldn't go *that* far."

"It's packed out there! I saw a dad threatening to make his kids play Monopoly if they didn't stop arguing."

"Did it work?"

"Oh yeah, right away. Those kids knew better than to ruin their big night out."

Eliza flashed a smile at him and filled four teapots with hot water. She loaded them onto a tray and held it up. "Do you mind carrying this for me?"

He was already reaching for it. "Not at all."

"Our game tonight is Cascadia – Mackenzie's choice. You win by building the best habitat for the animals. Bears, eagles... you get the idea."

"Sounds hard."

"It's not. It's fun, but I have to warn you. Mackenzie's competitive."

He followed her out to the London-themed tearoom, where a group had pushed two tables together for a sprawling game of Settlers of Catan.

"What about Cora?" he asked, placing the teapots down.

"She's more of a saboteur. Her favorite thing is to annoy Mackenzie. Luckily, you can't really do that in this game."

"Too bad. I would've liked to see it."

They returned to the kitchen just as a bell rang out – a request for a plate of cookies. Eliza didn't need his help, but he tagged along anyway and secured a lemon sugar cookie for his troubles.

This was the sort of business he could get behind. A cozy, laidback spot to hang out and drink tea.

He hadn't even liked tea before meeting Eliza. Like a fool, he thought the only tea out there was Lipton. There was an entire world of teas Eliza had introduced him to – fruity herbal teas, green teas, oolongs. Tonight, he was drinking pu-erh, a fermented variety Eliza made him try. He couldn't get enough.

"Well hello there!" Cora yelled as they approached the table. "Took you two long enough."

"People need their tea," Eliza said, taking a seat. "Joey, this is Cora, and—"

Cora thrust her hand forward. "I hear you're Eliza's partner in crime."

She had a delicate, cold grasp and an intense gaze. Her blonde hair was smooth and fluffed – what his sister called a blowout? Yeah, a blowout.

She wore a lot of makeup – red lipstick, black eyeliner, lots of shades of brown and glitter on her eyes. It fit with her nose ring and sequined shirt, but none of her seemed to fit with the rest of the tea shop – or Eliza, who didn't wear makeup at all.

Or maybe she did? He couldn't tell. Eliza was just pretty.

"Partners in crime," he mused. "I like that for us."

"I'm Mackenzie, Eliza's mean older sister." Mackenzie waved from her seat and made no attempt to smile.

"I've got a mean older sister of my own," he said, dropping into his chair. "I'm not afraid."

She didn't laugh, raising her eyebrows at him. "What made you decide to involve Eliza in your hunt for the bank robber?"

Eliza shot her an exasperated look. "You don't have to immediately interrogate him. He's not a threat."

Mackenzie looked at her and narrowed her eyes. "Everyone is a threat."

Eliza shook her head. "Don't mind her."

He smiled and poured himself a cup of tea. "I thought working with Eliza would give me the best chance at getting the reward money. I thought she'd be a good investigation partner."

"Smart," Cora said, nodding.

"But," he added, "I was wrong."

Cora dropped her teacup onto the saucer with a loud clang. "Sorry," she whispered.

"Do you guys want me to read the rules aloud?" Eliza asked, holding up the instructions to Cascadia.

Mackenzie waved a hand and leaned in. "What do you mean you were wrong?"

"Eliza's not a good partner." He took a sip of the tea. Excellent, as always. "She's an amazing partner."

Cora loudly sighed.

"Joey," Eliza said, her tone stern but her face hiding a smile. "Let's focus on the game, please."

"She remembered almost everything about the guy. The bank employees open up to her and tell her things they forgot to tell the police, and I'm convinced she's going to figure out his identity any day now."

"Interesting." Mackenzie sat back. "If she's so great at this, what does she need you for?"

He didn't miss a beat. "She's using me for my plane."

Eliza laughed. "I like the plane, but that's not it. Joey is the motivation. I wouldn't have done this on my own. He's sort of like an airborne cheerleader."

"Do you put on a little outfit, too?" Mackenzie asked with a smirk. "Pom-poms? Ribbons in your hair? I'd love to see it."

"So would I!" Cora said. "I mean, I want to go flying. I don't care what you wear."

"There aren't pom-poms, but I've got sunglasses. Does that count?"

Mackenzie shrugged. "It's not really the same at all."

"I'd be happy to take you up. We could—"

Eliza loudly cleared her throat. "Okay, everyone, we need to focus. We don't have all night."

"I have an idea," Mackenzie said. "Why don't we make this more interesting? Everyone put twenty dollars in. Whoever wins the game takes it all."

Cora bit her lip. "I don't know if I have twenty dollars." She pulled out her purse – the sequins matched the pink of her shirt – and came out with a pair of bills clutched in her hand. "Got it! I'm in!"

Joey pulled a twenty out of his wallet and offered it up as Eliza went through the rules.

Her rule-reading lasted for about three minutes before Cora started loudly whispering to Mackenzie.

"Have you talked to Steve at all?" she asked.

Mackenzie shook her head. "No."

"Who's Steve?" Joey whispered.

Eliza shot him an annoyed look but kept reading. "The way you are scored at the end...oh wait, I think I skipped a part..."

"Steve is my ex-boyfriend. Sort of." Mackenzie shifted her weight.

"They just broke up," Cora said. Her voice was more just a hoarse-sounding voice at normal volume than a whisper.

"I'm sorry to hear that," Joey whispered back.

"Thanks," Mackenzie said flatly, no longer trying to lower her voice. "Have you ever dated anyone? Or do you just fly around breaking hearts?"

He laughed mid-sip and threw himself into a coughing fit. "Sorry," he said when he regained his composure. "I never said anything about breaking hearts."

"I never took you for a romantic, Mack," Cora said.

"I'm not. My heart is only used to pump oxygen to my brain, so I'll remember to never loan you money."

Joey started choking again as Cora threw her head back and laughed.

For the first time, Eliza stopped reading. "Mackenzie! You have to at least try to be nice."

"No, it's okay." Cora held up her hand. "That was really funny. I love Mackenzie jokes. They're so brutal."

For the first time that night, Mackenzie smiled. "Thank you."

A bell rang out and Eliza stood. "Please look over the rest of the instructions so when I get back, we can get started."

"Sure," Mackenzie said, picking up the booklet.

"I'm glad Steve hasn't tried to talk to you," Cora said. "He's an idiot for what he did."

Mackenzie made a noncommittal noise, keeping her eyes on the booklet.

Joey looked at Cora and mouthed, "What did he do?"

"Did you tell his fiancée that he'd been two-timing you both?" Cora asked loudly.

Oh. Joey had not seen that coming. Mackenzie didn't seem like the type to get cheated on.

Not that there *was* a type, but he was surprised the guy was still standing.

"No," Mackenzie said. "I'm not sure how to do that without sounding like I'm jealous."

"Well, you're not jealous, so that would be on her for imagining it," Cora said simply. "He's a jerk."

"He is."

Eliza returned and took her seat. "Ready to start the game?"

"Do you believe in soulmates?" Cora asked Mackenzie.

She stared at the stack of cards on the table. "Absolutely not."

"Really? Why not?"

Mackenzie threw the booklet onto the table and started laying out the pieces for the game. "Because it's something made up by the diamond industry."

"Maybe you'll feel differently when you meet yours. Steve wasn't your soulmate." Cora turned to Joey. "What about you?"

"Believe in soulmates? Sure." He poured another cup of tea from the pot. "Steve still could've been her soulmate."

Mackenzie's narrowed eyes flashed up at him, her lip curled. "Are you serious?"

He went on. "Just because you don't end up together doesn't mean you weren't soulmates. Maybe some soulmates are supposed to show us how *not* to live our lives."

That had been his experience. There was a time when Joey had been a romantic. His girlfriend in college had given him a stuffed puffin after a trip they'd taken to Maine. The bright-billed birds had captured his imagination – they could fly at speeds over fifty miles an hour, dive two hundred feet into the ocean, and they mated for life.

He'd kept the little puffin on his bed, and his girlfriend started calling him Puff-Puff – sickeningly-sweet, but it didn't bother him. They were soulmates; he was sure of it.

He woke with only her on his mind and dreamt of her gentle smile when he slept. Joey could see their future as clear as a movie in his mind – their wedding, their coastal cottage with flowers spilling from the windows in the spring. He could feel the heat of the sun on his skin, he could smell the briny air.

"You might be on to something there," Mackenzie said, eyeing him. "Steve convinced me we were a power couple. After the same goals. It turns out he's a liar and a cheat and maybe a sociopath."

"Definitely a sociopath," Cora said with a nod.

"So I'm pretty sure I want nothing to do with the way he lives his life." She paused. "Or the way I was trying to live mine."

"See? Maybe next time you'll see it coming," Joey said. "You can leave before you're left."

Eliza took a deep breath and puffed out her cheeks. "This is turning into some sort of soulmate support group."

Mackenzie laughed. "No, it isn't. He couldn't have been my soulmate. How did I not realize that until Joey started pontificating?"

Though that was the exact opposite of what Joey had said, he smiled. "Happy to be of service."

His own soulmate had left him, and it was entirely due to his own mistakes. There was no wedding. No cottage. No flowers.

The breakup had left him heaving, completely empty, completely lost. He later found out there was some debate whether puffins did, in fact, mate for life. Though they returned to the same mate every year, it was possible they were only returning to the same burrow, and the particular bird waiting there didn't matter as much.

Joey had read on. He'd learned puffins spent more than half the year out at sea, alone, and realized the beautiful life he'd imagined was nothing more than a fantasy. One that wasn't meant for him.

He had to be completely gutted to see it, but once he did, he left, flying around the world, living his life the way he was supposed to: alone.

He looked up from his cup of tea. Eliza's eyes were focused on him, but she snapped them away, back to the booklet in her hand.

She cleared her throat. "Should we just start playing and I'll explain the rules as we go?"

It was hard to tell in the low lighting, but it looked like her cheeks were a little pink. Her stare was fixed on the booklet, allowing him a chance to look at her – the gentle slope of her nose, the curve of her lips...

His heart thudded against his ribs and his breathing picked up. Joey looked away, staring into his teacup.

This was not how his job on San Juan Island was supposed to go. The plan was to stay a few weeks, save some cash, and book his next adventure.

A few weeks might be too long. He glanced up at Eliza again. Thankfully, she was busy arguing with Cora about messing up the piles of tokens.

His hand shook as he reached for his teacup.

What was going on with him? He took a sip of tea, trying to steady his mind.

He knew this feeling. He used to chase it. He used to wake up with it, take it to dinner, dream with it under his pillow. But he'd managed to travel the world without running into it again – until this very moment.

What was it about Eliza that had brought it back to life? Was it the tea shop? The fact that if she gazed at him for too long, she could unravel him entirely and see every secret he'd desperately buried?

How would he get through the evening – even the next two minutes – without getting up from his seat and sprinting in the other direction?

"I'll go first," he said, picking up a token with a grizzly bear. "Or this game might never get started."

Fifteen

The game ended in such classic Dennet fashion that Mackenzie wanted to kick something. She'd thought she had a good chance at winning because Cora didn't understand the rules and Joey was too busy trying to be polite, but she'd forgotten about Eliza, quietly and steadily playing a near-perfect game and building the ideal planned habitat for her animals.

Why had Mackenzie picked a game with animals anyway? She thought she'd remembered how it worked, but it got cloudy after Cora started asking about Steve.

He had loved board games. He loved strategy. He was great to play with because he was clever and calculating.

Apparently, she hadn't known he applied that cold calculation to his life. Cutting her out was just part of the plan.

In true Eliza fashion, she humbly accepted her win and promptly handed her winnings to Cora.

"Don't give that to her!" Mackenzie hissed. "You won it fair and square."

"Yeah," Joey made a face. "Sorry, Cora, but you're one of us. A loser. You don't get to take the pot."

"It's not a big deal," Eliza said. "I could tell she really wanted to win, and she needs the money."

"I just couldn't make these stupid game hawks happy!" she whined. "Otherwise, I would've won."

"Yeah, and you didn't put the bears in pairs," Mackenzie pointed out. "Or the foxes in the right place at all."

Cora frowned and nodded. "All true, but listen. Now that I have some money, I can treat everyone to pizza tomorrow."

Eliza and Joey both groaned.

"Cora, please just keep the money for yourself," Eliza said. "You don't have to treat any of us."

"I'm sure Joey would like some pizza after he takes us up for a flight," she said, tucking the money into her pocket.

"I can't go up this week," Mackenzie said. "I have to do some work so I don't get fired."

"Getting fired is underrated," Cora said. "You should quit. Teach Steve a lesson."

Joey turned to her, his eyes wide. "He's your *boss?*"

"He got promoted," Mackenzie said quickly. "He's not just my boss. He's *her* boss, too."

Cora nodded. "He told her their relationship had to be secret because they worked together, but the whole time he was with the other—"

"Hey!" Mackenzie shot her a look. "How do you know all of this?"

Eliza cut in. "I'm sorry, I told her." She turned toward Cora and lowered her voice. "*So she wouldn't ask too many questions.*"

Cora winced. "Sorry! I just feel bad for you."

"Don't worry about me," Mackenzie said, loading the game pieces back into their velvet bags. She had to blink to clear her vision. All the crying had done something to her tear ducts. It felt like her eyelids dragged across her eyeballs, sinking them further in their sockets. "I'm fine."

Joey stood from his seat. "It was lovely hanging out with you ladies tonight, but I've got to get going. I have early flights tomorrow morning."

"Bye bye, Joey. Fly safe!" Cora said, waving him off.

"Have a good night," Eliza said.

He smiled at her. "I'll text you."

Ooh la la. Mackenzie sat cleaning up the pieces, a little smile on her face. She kept waiting for Eliza to make eye contact with her so she could say something, but she never did. Her eyes followed Joey, lingering on the front door long after he was gone.

Mackenzie sat back and crossed her arms. She'd fully expected Joey to detract from their evening, but she was pleasantly surprised with how unoffensive he was. He had that unaffected, aloof charm the girls went wild for.

He was cute, too. Not Mackenzie's type, but it seemed he might be Eliza's type.

Mackenzie packed the bags and cards neatly into the box. "Are you in love with him?" she asked.

Eliza spat out a laugh. "What? No."

"He's pretty dreamy," Cora said, a twinkle in her eye. "I can tell you like him."

Eliza stood, fussing with the game pieces, straightening them out. "Well, yeah, he's easy to like, but it doesn't matter. It's not romantic. It's professional."

"Aw, why not?" Cora asked. "He seems like he likes you. He makes excuses to see you."

"Yeah," Eliza rolled her eyes. "Probably because he thinks this island is a retirement community like you do and there's no one else to hang out with."

Cora shook her head. "I take that back. There are plenty of young people here. It's a vibrant community, indeed."

Eliza raised her eyebrows. "I'm glad you see it that way."

"Do you like him?" Mackenzie asked.

She'd been half joking, but Joey probably did fly around breaking hearts. What if he was a player? How would Eliza even find out? He could be ten times worse than Steve—a girl-friend in every city! Every country!

"I'm not delusional enough to think he'd ever go for some-one like me," Eliza said softly. "We're just friends. There's nothing more to it than that."

A bell rang out and Eliza stood to tend to it.

Mackenzie blinked hard, dragging her stiff, dry eyelids over her scratchy eyes. "I, for one, am glad she's not into him. He seems like a risky choice."

"Oh." Cora sunk into her chair. "I'm sad for her."

"Don't be." Mackenzie had to hold her tongue. Cora was like a plastic bag caught in the wind. She didn't understand what was going on in front of her. "It's for the best."

"She never thinks anyone likes her. She thinks she's unlikable."

"That's ridiculous, Eliza can't think that. She's not unlikable." Mackenzie shrugged. "He's probably just a playboy and she's better off staying away."

"I don't know about that. She clearly likes him, and Eliza tends to be a good judge of character." Cora paused. "I know you're speaking from your experience and you don't want her to be fooled, but there's no indication that he's up to no good. He seems like a nice guy."

Mackenzie hadn't heard Cora make that coherent of a statement all night.

Even if she was wrong.

She crossed her arms. "I'm guessing you would tell me I missed a bunch of warning signs with Steve? That I should've known he was lying to me and had another girl on the side?"

Cora put her hands up. "No! Every act of love is an act of courage. We can be careful, but we can't completely avoid risk."

"Then that's it. Eliza is being careful with him. I think that's good."

"I don't think that's it. Eliza doesn't think she's good enough for anyone. She thinks she has to be perfect to deserve love."

This tea was making her nauseated. It was too lemony. It was like reflux in a cup. Mackenzie set it down. "Why are you saying all of this?"

Cora, who had been staring into space, startled and looked at her. "I thought you knew. She's always been like this."

"Of course I knew! She's *my* sister."

"I'm not accusing you of anything." Cora sighed. "I'm her best friend. I've seen her at her lowest. Eliza tries to look strong for everyone."

The heat rose from her chest and into her throat. "So she tries to look strong for me, but she's willing to be vulnerable and tell you all these things?"

"I'm not trying to compete with you," Cora said gently. "Eliza doesn't have to worry about looking bad in front of me."

Mackenzie scoffed. That was true.

"Though I know she still tries to be strong," Cora added. "I'm so much of a mess, I don't make anyone feel self-conscious."

Mackenzie let out a breath and uncrossed her arms. "You're not a mess."

"Oh no, I really am." She drew herself up and took a deep breath. "I just wish Eliza didn't spend so much time measuring herself, thinking she's supposed to be this, or supposed to be that, and always finding herself lacking. It makes me sad. She's incredible and she doesn't see it."

Mackenzie looked down at her hands. She'd never considered that Cora might care so much for Eliza. Mackenzie tended to get stuck on the whole ditzy-rich girl thing. "She's a perfectionist."

"I know. That's the thing about perfectionists. They don't believe they have any worth if they're not impossibly exceptional."

Impossibly exceptional. The words landed on Mackenzie's chest with a punch. The heat on her skin dissipated, blasted away. "And you think Eliza believes pilot boy is too good for her?"

"She thinks every guy is too good for her. Have you ever seen her with a boyfriend?"

"There was that one guy. He was...interesting." She scrunched her nose. "He always smelled."

"He did, didn't he?" Cora shook her head. "And he never did anything nice for her. He only thought of himself. He was so...disappointing."

Her breath stung in her throat. She took a sip of water.

How had she not noticed any of this about her own sister? Mackenzie hadn't put nearly as much thought into analyzing it as Cora had. Until this moment, Mackenzie had written her off as a self-absorbed simpleton.

Who was the simpleton now?

"Can we help her?" Mackenzie asked.

"Oh, sure." Cora smiled. "Just keep loving her."

For the first time, Mackenzie had something more important to think about than her own broken heart.

It was the best she'd felt in weeks.

She nodded and picked up her cup of reflux tea. "You and me, Cora. We're going to crack this one. For Eliza."

Cora raised her cup. "For Eliza!"

Sixteen

After convincing the last table of patrons to continue their game at home, Eliza finished cleaning the tea shop with Mackenzie and Cora's help.

The night of fun had done something for Mackenzie. She was no longer jabbing at Cora, instead moving on to gentle teasing.

"I've always thought you were a real-life Elizabeth Bennet," Mackenzie mused as she wiped the tables. "Your choice of best friend brings that into question."

"I may not be as practical as Charlotte Lucas," Cora said, packing up the leftover cookies, "but I am still an excellent best friend."

Eliza smiled to herself. "Did you finally get around to reading *Pride and Prejudice*?"

Mackenzie sighed. "I don't have time for that."

Cora gasped. "What do you even know about Charlotte Lucas? I would totally marry your creepy cousin to save Eliza."

"That's not exactly what happened," Eliza said, balancing a tray on her hip.

"You know what, Mackenzie," Cora said slowly. "You remind me a bit of Charlotte Lucas."

"*Me?*" She scoffed. "I'm not some simpering fool who would marry her cousin out of desperation."

Cora threw her hands up. "It's not Charlotte's cousin, it's Eliza's cousin! Don't you know her famous line from the movie? It's totally you."

"I highly doubt that," Mackenzie said.

"She's like, 'I'm twenty-seven! I don't have any money and I'm a burden to my parents! I'm scared! Don't look at me!'"

Eliza frowned. That wasn't the quote, but it was close enough for the two of them. They erupted into laughter.

"Wait, *I'm* twenty-seven!" Mackenzie said, covering her face with her hands. "Is Charlotte really twenty-seven in the movie?"

"She is," Eliza said. "Coincidentally, you are a burden to your parents."

Mackenzie laughed harder and Eliza got sucked in, too.

Outside of the tea shop, waves exploded in the darkness and crashed on the shore. Inside, there was nothing but the warm glow of the lights and their snorting laughter.

It took them a while to recover, but Mackenzie finally managed to change the subject. "What's the next step in your robbery investigation?"

The wet rag in her hands stung Eliza's skin. There were cracks in her fingers from always washing dishes. She needed to remember to moisturize. "I'm not sure. Joey said he has some free time on Monday so we could fly to see more of the bank branches, but I've got to be at the tea shop."

Cora's face brightened. "Let me take over! If you tell me a few details, I think I can keep the ship afloat."

"No, that's okay. I don't want you to have to do that."

"Please." Cora's eyes were wide. "I *need* you to solve this mystery."

Eliza tried not to smile. "Can you imagine how crazy it would be to find the guy? Maybe everyone would stop thinking I'm such an idiot for helping him rob the bank."

"You're not an idiot," Mackenzie said firmly. "I think you're capable of finding him, but you don't have to find him. You don't have to prove anything to anyone. We love you just the way you are."

Eliza pulled back. "Where did that come from?"

She shrugged. "I'm channeling Charlotte Lucas."

"Don't start that again," Eliza said. "If I laugh any more, I think I'll fall over."

"Fine, but listen. You seem to have fun with Joey, so why not go and have some fun?" Mackenzie said. "I can help Cora too."

"Are you sure?" Eliza studied her. "I know you have a lot to catch up on after taking off work."

Mackenzie waved a hand. "The longer I'm away, the clearer things become. I'm not even sure I still want to work there."

"Wow. Okay. Maybe you've been talking to Cora too much."

"Maybe. Now say yes before I change my mind."

Cora squealed. "Yes! Say yes!"

"Well..."

She didn't want to miss a chance to spend more time with Joey. They could be hunting for Bigfoot for all she cared. Sunsets always came too quickly...

A smile crept onto her face. "If you insist."

. . .

Their first stop on Monday was in Anacortes. It was one of the later robberies where the thief had cleaned out the ATM. He had hardly interacted with the staff, and they stood no chance of recognizing him – he'd hit the branch on Halloween dressed in a full Darth Vader costume, complete with a glowing lightsaber.

Joey still thought it was worth it to talk to them. "You tend to get information out of people that they didn't even think of before."

Eliza looked down at her hands. She was getting more used to flying in the plane, but compliments from him still made her stomach flip. Not that she wanted it to stop...

"I think I got lucky last time. It's not like I'm doing anything useful with this information. Some of it doesn't even make sense. Like the teller at the last bank who told me she felt the robber was a pirate in his past life."

A half-smile crossed his face and he looked at her from the corner of his eye. "You haven't figured out how to put it all together yet, but I have faith."

She shook her head and turned to hide her smile. Who knew what would happen? Beneath the plane, the world was open, stretches of blue cut with jagged islands rising in spikes and peaks. It was a different view than from the ferry, but once she had gotten past her terrifying visions of falling into the sea, she loved it just as much.

They landed in Anacortes and caught a ride to the bank. Eliza had tried calling ahead to talk to the manager, but she never got through to him and he didn't reply to her email.

When they met him in person, it became clear his silence had been intentional.

"Listen here," he said, eyes narrowed as he barreled out of his office. "I haven't got time for another enthusiast who wants to play cops and robbers. If you're customers of the bank and have business here, that's one thing. If you're here because you think of yourselves as amateur sleuths, get out or I will call the police."

He stopped inches away from Joey's face, staring him in the eye.

"Well then." Joey gently bowed forward, nearly bumping the manager in the forehead. "I guess you don't want to hear about our exciting timeshare opportunity, either?"

"Get out! Now!" the man bellowed.

Eliza jumped. "Sorry!"

She rushed outside. If only she could crawl out of her skin and swim back to San Juan Island. Then she'd never have to face Joey or his overinflated faith in her again.

She didn't have any special skills in talking to people or getting them to open up. She'd gotten lucky and that one lady was really talkative and—

Joey broke the silence. "What a jerk."

"Yeah." She bit her lip. "Maybe we should go home. I don't want him to report us to the ATF."

"Forget him!" Joey waved a hand. "He's just crabby. They probably have too many people coming to talk to them because of the reward."

"Right. Which is exactly what we're doing."

"We're not just in it for the reward," he said. "We're also trying to restore your honor."

She snorted. "My honor? Has it been besmirched?"

"It has been besmirched, Lady Dennet."

Eliza laughed. "If you're trying to talk like a Jane Austen character, you're failing."

He frowned. "I don't know how I'm supposed to fix that."

"You could try reading a book."

"I can't read."

She cracked a smile. "I thought you'd have to be able to read to become a pilot."

"You'd think that," he said, slipping his sunglasses on, "but I've found a way around it on pure wit and charm."

She raised an eyebrow. "Interesting."

"I have an idea."

"Was it built with wit and charm?" she asked.

"Yes," he said curtly. "How about this? We head to Bellingham and I'll go into the branch to feel it out. Let me do the talking and, if the manager is friendly, I'll send you a signal."

"Like a text?"

"Yeah."

She made a face. "I thought you couldn't read?"

A smile inched onto his face, the dimple starting to form. "It'll be a picture of me giving a thumbs-up."

She stared at him. "And I'm supposed to wait outside and try to not look suspicious?"

"Yes! Glad to see you're on board." He held out his arm. "My lady?"

"I'm not agreeing to this plan," she said with a sigh, walking past him. "I'd like to go home."

He took his sunglasses off, raising his eyebrows and widening his eyes. "Please?"

Her chest expanded, her heart collapsing into a puddle. There was no way for her to say no to that face.

"Okay," she said weakly, taking his arm.

The flight to Bellingham was a short one, but long enough for Eliza to pull herself together. Joey talked the entire time, telling her a story about how he'd almost stolen a plane.

It had been a mistake – an unscrupulous business owner had tried to trick him into taking the wrong plane from an airfield and Joey was blissfully unaware until the last second.

All Eliza could think was that it wasn't much different than what was happening now. He had no idea what was going on between them. He thought they were partners? Friends?

All the while, she turned to mush with just a look.

Not that she'd ever say anything. It was better he didn't know. It would probably make him uncomfortable and he'd have to have the inevitable "I value you as a friend" talk with her. Then, every time they passed at the tea shop, she'd have to pretend not to see him. Try to keep herself from staring from afar as he told his charming stories to other women...

When they landed, she shut her thoughts into a little compartment and followed him all the way to the Bellingham bank branch.

Less than ten minutes after he went inside, Eliza got a text with his picture, as promised. In it, he was grinning and giving a thumbs up, along with the suited woman behind him.

He really was ridiculous.

She went inside and was greeted immediately by the manager, an attractive woman in a perfectly fitted green suit.

"You kind of remind me of the robber, you know," she said to Joey. "Tall. Handsome. In charge."

Eliza leaned in, eyebrows furrowed. "Oh?"

"I like to think I have *some* things going for me," Joey said. "I don't know why you sound so surprised."

Eliza couldn't tell if he was playing dumb. She laughed. "I'm not questioning you being handsome. I'm questioning the bank robber being handsome." She turned back to the manager. "So you got a good look at him?"

"No, not really. He had a ski mask over his face, but he looked, you know. In shape. Muscles. And he had good hands. Do you know what I mean?"

Eliza nodded. "I do know what you mean."

"What are good hands?" Joey asked. "Do I have good hands?"

Eliza and the manager both glanced at him and replied, "Yes."

Joey held his hands out in front of him. "Who knew?"

"Can you focus for one second?" Eliza asked.

Grinning, he put his hands in his pockets. "Yes. Sorry. It's not every day you find out you've got good hands."

Eliza tried to keep the smile off her face and turned back to the manager. "Did he have any tattoos or scars?"

She shook her head. "He only took his gloves off for a moment, but he looked strong. Big forearms, you know?" She nodded at Joey. "Like you. Do you work with your hands?"

Was it possible for her eyes to roll all the way into the back of her head?

Joey shook his head. "No. I'm a pilot."

"A pilot. Fascinating." She leaned in. "Did you fly here?"

He shrugged. "We did, yeah."

She looked him up and down. "Well, anytime you're in the area again, please come and pay me a visit. I *love* to fly."

"Sure," Joey said with a nod. "Thanks for talking with us. If you think of anything else..."

"Write down your number," she said, handing him a business card. "I'll get in touch."

"Sure."

"Excuse me," Eliza said, "can I get one of those?"

She pulled out another business card and handed it over without making eye contact. "Of course."

Pretty hair, perfect makeup, an expensive-looking outfit. She seemed like the kind of woman Joey should be with. Eliza watched as he jotted down his phone number. There was no use being jealous. This was the natural state of things.

She shoved the card into her back pocket and turned to leave. He caught up with her outside.

"Looks like you're not the only one people like opening up to," he said, a smirk on his face.

"I don't want to ever hear you claim I'm good with people again," Eliza snapped. "I think she was about to give you the key to her house."

A laugh burst out of him. "That was weird, wasn't it?"

"I'm surprised she didn't ask the bank robber out, too."

"I bet she did but he turned her down."

She cracked a smile. "That's probably what happened."

Joey's phone rang – Russell asking if he could stop by Anacortes to pick up his stranded agent.

"No problem. We're really close." He ended the call and made a face. "Do you mind?"

"Not at all. I'll sit in the back. You won't even notice me."

"Are you sure? You won't be able to see my good hands from there."

She shook her head. "I'm never telling you anything ever again."

He laughed. "You don't mean it."

They returned to the plane and Eliza planted herself in the back seat. She was happy to have a different view and a chance to be alone with her thoughts.

Though it was disturbing how much the bank manager seemingly had the hots for the robber, it was insightful. Eliza had assumed he was older, but she had based that off his pretending to be frail when she met him.

He wasn't some wise old bank robber – he was a young guy. Strong, apparently, with big forearms.

Eliza hadn't seen that in his oversized leather jacket. What else had she missed? What else had she assumed?

Russell's agent got onto the plane, taking a seat in the front. Eliza said hello but otherwise kept to herself, still daydreaming, her mind interrogating the memories she had from that day.

They were back in the air in no time. Eliza leaned over, looking at the islands below, when she felt something pressing into her back. She shoved her hand between the seat cushions and pulled out the offending object: a brown leather tassel with gold thread.

She gasped.

"Everything okay?" Joey asked, his eyes darting back at her.

She shoved the tassel under her leg. "Good, yeah."

There was no mistaking it. The golden thread, the dash of pink – this was the robber's tassel.

Why was it in Joey's plane?

Seventeen

The sea pen kept building momentum. Joey spent half his time flying Hollywood people to and from Seattle, and one had even asked if he could "drop him off in LA," as if it were as easy as popping over a few mountains.

The flights were endless, looping back and forth like the thoughts in his mind. They circled the same thing, the same person. The same set of eyes.

On game night, he was sure Eliza had looked at him a certain way. That her intense gaze had lingered, that there was *something* behind those mysterious eyes.

He'd braced himself for their trip to Anacortes a few days later, sure she'd betray some sentiment he'd have to shoot down in the interest of their robber search, but bafflingly, she acted completely normal. She had no jealousy when the bank manager tried to flirt with him, going as far as to scoff at the whole thing.

It hit him like a goose getting sucked into a plane's engine. Eliza hadn't been looking at him any special way that night. She didn't feel anything for him.

It was *him*. He was the one with the feelings.

He was the one with the problem.

Joey flew back and forth, circling this undeniable fact. It should have made him upset, but it made him feel like he was getting away with something.

Spending time with Eliza was a thrill. Every smile, every laugh sent a zing down his spine. He was the proverbial moth near the flame, close without having to risk being sucked in.

The perfect situation – until their last flight, when Eliza told him they should take a break from investigating.

"I feel like we're not getting anywhere," she said when they landed. "And I have guests here now and..."

His heart sank. "We can't give up! We're getting closer."

"Not give up," she said slowly. "Just take a break."

Eliza opened the plane door and hopped out.

"A break?" Every step she took away from him only pulled him in closer. "I can take a break. Just promise you won't figure out who the robber is without telling me."

She flashed a smile over her shoulder. "Yeah, ha. No way."

Joey had to believe that it was a break and not an end to their search. Otherwise, he'd have no way to get through the dull conversations with Russell's celebrity friends.

The only person who was excited by all the Hollywood hullabaloo was Cora. She asked to spend a day with him to try to rub elbows with "the rich and fabulous."

"Maybe I'll get discovered! That's what happened to Russell, you know. They just plucked him out of a crowd and voilà!"

That probably wasn't how it went down, but Joey wasn't going to say anything. If he could make Cora happy, maybe she'd help at the tea shop again so Eliza could have a day off.

He took her up on a Friday morning. Cora sat in the front and within the first thirty minutes, he had to yell at her four times to keep her hands off the control panel.

Their first trip was flying Russell's agent back to Seattle. Cora peppered him with questions.

"Who's the worst person you've had to work with?"

He laughed. "Like I'm going to tell you."

"Good point." She pointed at him. "Who was the best, then?"

"Russell, obviously."

She groaned. "You're no fun."

"Fun doesn't pay the bills," he said.

This seemed to hit Cora and she sat back, quiet for a moment. "You are so right. Fun *doesn't* pay the bills."

They dropped him off before he had a chance to discover Cora and her special talent – whatever that was – and on their flight back, Cora turned to questioning him.

"Tell me, Joey. You seemed to have a pretty developed theory about soulmates. What's your dating history?"

"My dating history? You want a full rundown or something?"

She waved a hand. "You know what I mean. Your greatest love story, Joey. Don't jerk me around."

This was a first. People didn't normally ask him questions. He was much better with listening. He'd probably make a great podcast host, if he ever found the time. "I had a love story once. A girl I dated in college."

"Do tell! What was she like? What happened?"

"There's not much to say. She was perfect. I was madly in love, I messed it up, and that was that."

"What do you mean, there's not much to say? You made me think of a hundred more questions."

"Er, yeah. I should've seen that coming."

She gawked at him, mouth open. "Wait a minute. Are you a Steve?"

Their relationship had ended so badly it had made him fly to the other side of the world. So... "I guess. Yeah, I was a Steve."

"What! You're a cheater?" She smacked his arm.

"Ow!" He pulled away, rubbing his shoulder. "No hitting the pilot!"

"Steve status trumps pilot status," Cora said, eyes narrowed.

"I'm not a cheater! I thought you meant a Steve was a disappointing boyfriend." He shouldn't have brought this up. Maybe he wasn't cut out to be a podcast host after all. "I don't think you want to hear this story."

"More like you don't want to tell me."

She wasn't wrong. He glanced at her, but quickly looked away. "It's not the best in-air story."

She leaned in closer. "I don't care. Tell me."

She was inches from his face, her lips pursed and her eyes narrowed.

He flinched, pressing his body against the door. "All right! We were dating for a year and I was madly in love. I took her up for a flight, planning to propose."

She gasped. "A year!"

"Yes. I was that young and dumb."

"Romantic," she corrected.

Yeah, right. Romantic. He shook his head. "I really wanted to do it on our one-year anniversary, but the weather wasn't cooperating. I shouldn't have taken her up, but I was too stubborn to change my plans. We got into the air and within five minutes, we were back down. Crashed into a forest."

"You *killed* her, Joey? Are you kidding me! You are way worse than a Steve!"

"I didn't kill her!" He sighed. He couldn't even talk without her jumping down his throat. "She survived. She's fine."

Cora frowned. "Oh."

Maybe telling stories wasn't his forte after all. It'd been so long since he'd shared this particular story with anyone. He should've kept it that way.

It was too late now. He went on. "I never lost consciousness, but she did. I crawled out of the wreckage to get help. When she woke up, I wasn't there."

Joey took a deep breath and closed his eyes. The image of that dark afternoon flashed in his mind, the rumble of the storm, the smell of burning plastic, and the cool, wet ground of the forest.

"She woke up and thought I'd abandoned her. Never forgave me."

Cora was quiet. "But she survived?"

"Yeah."

"Was she hurt?"

Other than thinking her boyfriend had abandoned her in the wreckage of his own mistakes?

Because he had. Even if it was only for a moment, he'd left her there. His first thought should have been to pull her out, check her breathing.

"Fractured arm and clavicle."

"What about you?" Cora put her hand on his shoulder. "Other than your broken heart?"

A pit opened in his stomach. This was taking a turn, one he had no interest in.

Joey pulled his shoulder away from her grasp. "I'm sorry. This isn't personal, but I'm not interested in anything. You know, between us."

Her mouth popped open. "Ew, I'm not interested in you! Get over yourself!"

"I'm sorry!" He put his hands up. "You just touched me, and I wanted to be clear."

"I would never do that to Eliza."

Joey stopped and turned to look at her. "Eliza?"

She clapped a hand over her mouth. "I shouldn't have said that."

"What does you touching me have to do with Eliza?"

A smile crept onto his face. He'd been wrong after all.

Was she playing hard to get? Or was she that focused on finding the robber?

Cora sighed and rolled her eyes. "Don't play dumb."

"Are you saying...she likes me?"

"I didn't say that!" she snapped. "You and Eliza clearly have a *thing* going on, and I'd never do that to my best friend."

He raised an eyebrow. "So...she has a crush on me."

"Are you really that dense? Do you not have eyes?"

A laugh sputtered out of him. "I don't normally stick around long enough to have women interested in me, to be honest."

"Just the one you almost got killed."

He winced. Cora was sharper than he'd given her credit for. "Actually, yeah. She was the last one."

"The last one you ever loved?"

"The only one I ever loved."

Cora put the back of her hand to her forehead. "Oh, how could you ever love again after that?"

And she was more annoying than he'd realized. "It's just – you don't understand."

"Yes, I do." She laughed. "I see right through you." She raised a hand and flicked him in the ear.

"Ow!" He recoiled. "What did I say about hitting the pilot?"

"You're not a Steve. Not at all. You believe in soulmates and ill-advised proposals."

"One could argue Steve's proposal was ill-advised. For Mackenzie."

Cora made a face. "True."

Joey didn't like talking about this as much as he'd thought he would. Time to change the subject.

"What about you? Who was your one true love?"

"One?" She shook her head. "Where do I begin?"

It worked like a charm. Cora talked about herself for the rest of the flight while Joey got to sit and listen.

Still, his listening was impaired. His mind kept drifting to what Cora had said about Eliza.

Technically, she'd never outright said Eliza was interested in him. She told him to use his eyes.

What did he see when he looked at Eliza? Someone who had no interest in spending time with him. Someone who had put their search on hold.

Eliza didn't like him. She couldn't. Even if she did, it wouldn't matter. The contract Joey had signed with Russell was only for a few weeks. He had the option to renew, but why should he? He'd made enough money to go lay on the beach in Bali, or dive into the thermal baths in Budapest, or get an apartment with a view of the Seine.

Joey had a great love once, yes. That had been all it was – a one-time thing. It taught him a lot, mainly that he wasn't the type to love. He was the type to go out and take the world for all it was worth. He was happy with that. Comfortable with it.

They approached San Juan Island from above. He tried to drown out Cora's babbling and focus on the plane's gauges instead of the fact that when he pictured Eliza's smile, his heart jumped.

Eighteen

The tassel rolled in Eliza's hand, light catching on the fine gold thread. It was real, and it had come from the robber's hat. She was sure of it.

What she wasn't sure of was why Joey had it in his plane. She had ideas, of course.

Maybe he'd found it on the ground and thought it looked pretty. Maybe he collected tassels for fun. Or he might have worked with the robber, helping him escape the island by seaplane, just as the rumors had whispered.

There was, of course, a chance that the charming pilot who had fallen out of the sky to tell her she was the only one who might be able to catch the robber could, in fact, be the robber.

Not that she believed any of that. Not intellectually.

Just in her gut and in her heart, which raced through the night, leaving her staring at the ceiling as Mackenzie snored.

Eliza hated secrets. She hated wondering. Years ago, when her parents were getting divorced, when her life was severed into a *before* and an *after*, she found out something she shouldn't have.

Though her parents had said they'd fallen out of love and the divorce was mutual, the truth was that her dad had been having an affair. What was more shocking – her mother had known for months.

Months! Eliza was sure she'd never understand it. How could her mom put up with that? Why didn't she confront him? Confront *her?* Tell the world and scare this interloper off and save their family?

There was a touch of juvenile naivety there. Eliza knew that, but she couldn't fathom why her mom had kept quiet about it all that time.

Until now. As soon as she'd found the tassel, she should have called Stacy, the mean ATF agent. She should have told the police. At the very least, she should have told Mackenzie. (But not Cora. She couldn't keep a secret to save her life).

Instead, she went to work at the tea shop as if nothing had happened, keeping the tassel in her pocket, checking on it now and again, only daring to look at it when she was sure she was alone.

For the rest of the week, she gave Joey excuses as to why she couldn't see him. She told Cora and Mackenzie she was busy working on a website update for the tea shop and didn't have much time to spend with them, either.

It worked. Mackenzie, had she not been in the process of getting fired from her job, might have noticed. Cora didn't buy her lie for a second, but she was too busy trying to get discovered to pry.

It gave Eliza time to think, time to argue with herself. Her mind was vindicated. *See? I knew he couldn't be into you. He just wanted to see if you'd figured him out. If you confront him, he's going to toss you out of the plane to be swallowed by the sea.*

Her heart was another story. It had hope, and she knew a hopeful heart would make a fool of her.

She didn't tell anyone, but used that hope to pluck up the courage to return to the scene of the crime.

Despite the island being only fifty-five square miles, she'd managed to avoid going anywhere near the bank. Cora agreed to cover the tea shop, and Eliza made the trip.

Driving there now was just as bad as she'd imagined. Sweat pooled on her top lip and her hands shook as she pulled into the parking lot.

"There's no truck today. There's no bank robber," she repeated to herself.

What if Mackenzie was right? What if no one could be trusted? What if you could never truly know someone?

She pulled into a spot and muttered, "The bank robber isn't here because he's probably busy flying around."

Could Joey be so cold-blooded to sit around, drinking tea and laughing, all while goading her into finding the criminal he knew to be himself?

Being at the bank wasn't as bad as being in her mind. She shuddered and got out of the car.

She walked inside and one of the tellers spotted her immediately.

"Eliza!" The teller smiled and waved. "How are you?"

"I'm good," she said, trying to steady her voice. "How are you?"

"Oh, you know. Having nightmares about bombs. No big deal."

Eliza nodded. "I hear you."

The manager, a middle-aged woman in a cardigan and high-waisted pants, emerged her office and greeted Eliza with a handshake. "I was wondering when you'd come back, or if you ever would."

"To be honest, I didn't think I could do it." She stopped herself. "I'm sorry, I know you had it much worse. I slept through most of the robbery."

The manager laughed. "Please, let's not compare trauma. We're doing okay here. The bank sent a counselor to talk to all of us. Have you talked to anyone?"

Just to the bank robber, day in and day out. "No."

"Come with me. Do you want some tea? Water?"

"Tea would be nice."

She stopped at an electric kettle and made up two cups of Earl Grey before leading the way to her office.

Eliza cleared her throat. "This is going to sound silly, but I've been trying to learn more about the robbery."

A smile crossed her face. "Hoping to get the reward?"

"It's not just that. I'm trying to reclaim some of my dignity."

And sanity, though that seemed like a lost cause.

"Your dignity!" The manager snorted a laugh. "Oh, stop. No one understands how scary it is to be in that sort of a situation. I can't count how many people told me how they would've handled it better than I did."

Eliza smiled. She took a sip of tea and the tension loosed from her muscles. "I've had a similar experience."

"I'm happy to help in any way I can, but to be honest, he wasn't here much longer than you were." She set her tea down. "After you fainted, he took a few thousand dollars from us, emptied the ATM, and drove off in his truck. He didn't leave anything behind."

Eliza frowned. "What did he seem like to you? Charming? Funny?" *Good at flying?*

The manager looked up at the ceiling, biting her lip. "If I had to put it in a word, I'd say professional."

It was her first time hearing that. "Really."

"He knew what he was doing, as in he was sure of every action. I know he's robbed banks before, but it was something else." She shook her head. "I told this to the police, but I think he either works in our banks or knows someone who does."

Eliza raised an eyebrow. "That's interesting."

"I thought so, but the agent interviewing me thanked me for my 'astute conjecture' and said to leave it to the professionals."

Now it was Eliza's turn to laugh. "Was it Agent Stacy? Skinny with long dark hair?"

"Yeah, that's the one."

At least Eliza wasn't the only one Stacy was mean to. That was a small comfort. "She thought I was involved in the robbery, and I was playing dumb." Eliza leaned in. "I cannot stress this enough: I *swear* I had nothing to do with it. I'm so sorry I helped him walk in here. I was afraid to show my face again...I'll never live it down."

The manager waved a hand. "Please, don't apologize! He was coming to rob the bank with or without you. It wasn't your fault. Don't beat yourself up about it."

This woman was so nice. And sort of cool. She reminded her of her mom. "I came to the bank that day to ask about a student loan that day. Not to rob it."

Her smile brightened. "Well, why don't I help you with that? We can get back on track."

"Right now?"

She turned to her computer. "There's no time like the present."

Eliza sighed. "If you say so."

. . .

Filling out the loan application made her feel like the trip to the bank was worth it, even if she hadn't learned anything new. Afterward, she drove into town to pick up frozen puff pastry – it was cheating, but she didn't have the patience to fold in all that butter herself – and decided to stop by her favorite coffee shop.

As she walked in, the memory of visiting with Joey hit her with a wave of nausea. He'd pretended to know nothing about the wheelchair that day.

How could he do that? How could he be so convincing? What else was he capable of?

She pushed the memory out of her mind and walked up to the counter. "Hey, Wally."

"Eliza! How's it going? Did you find that wheelchair you were looking for?"

"Oh," she said slowly. "I don't think he'll be needing it anymore."

"That's good, because someone threw it away."

"What? Why?"

He shrugged his shoulders. "We got a fine for having an overflowing dumpster. Turns out someone threw the wheelchair in there. We caught them on video, but no one recognized them."

She swallowed. This could be it, the evidence she needed to prove it was Joey. "Can I see it?"

"Sure. Come on back."

He led her to the storage room where a black laptop sat idle. Sweat slid down her back and she stood, trying to control her breathing.

"Here you go." He spun the screen around and clicked play. "You can't really make out who it is. Well, maybe you can. I can't."

Eliza leaned in and watched a hooded figure in a black jacket dragging the wheelchair behind the dumpster. They struggled to close it, then to throw it into the dumpster. The person's face briefly flashed at the camera in a blur.

"Have you shown this to the police?" Eliza asked, trying to freeze the frame on the person's face.

"Nah. Grace didn't want to deal with it and it was her wheelchair. I just thought it was strange."

She zoomed in on the face and, at first, her mind refused to absorb what was in front of her.

She had expected to see Joey – his chiseled features, his ever-laughing mouth – but it wasn't him. It was a lady, dark hair pouring out of her hoodie.

Eliza should have felt relief, but curiously, the nausea was back in full force.

"Do you know her?" Wally asked.

Eliza stood, straightening her back. "No," she lied, eyes lingering on Agent Stacy's face. "I wish I could help."

"Don't worry about it. Do you want a matcha latte?"

"Yeah," she said. "That'd be great."

Nineteen

Though Mackenzie didn't agree with it, she sort of admired Cora's determination to get discovered.

They were all sitting in the kitchen, drinking tea, when she stomped in and insisted Russell record her audition video.

"An audition for what?" he asked.

"For whatever someone thinks I'd be good at!" she snapped, smoothing her hair with one hand and giving him her phone with the other. "It's set up to record. Action!"

They erupted into laughter, and every attempt thereafter was ruined by either Granny, Mom, Eliza, or Mackenzie breaking into giggles.

Russell even ruined one take, trying so hard to hold in his laughter that his hand shook, ruining the shot.

Cora was undeterred. She thanked him for his help before going back upstairs to pack.

"I'm glad it's over. I can't laugh anymore," Mackenzie said, rubbing her face.

"Do you want me to shoot your video next?" Russell asked.

There was nothing Mackenzie would like less. "No. Hollywood seems too much like everything I don't like about my current job."

Eliza frowned. "How is being a tech saleswoman the same as being an actress?"

"It's just people, Eliza." Mackenzie smiled. She sounded like Cora. "Sales lacks some of the glamour – the red carpets, the fawning interviews, the designer dresses – but not all the glamour. There are still big egos and big paychecks. People get crazy."

"Like Steve," Mom hissed, narrowing her eyes. "I've got a mind to give him a call. Did you remember he sent me flowers on my birthday?"

"Steve the snake," Eliza said, shaking her head.

Mackenzie grabbed an oatmeal cookie and shoved it in her mouth. "I heard someone saw a snake on the tea shop patio."

Granny gasped, looking down at the fluffy Golden Retriever at her feet. "Derby! You're supposed to alert me to any new animal visitors!"

He looked up at her, his ears back, and panted a Golden smile.

She patted him on the head. "I know your hearing isn't what it used to be. You'll get the next one."

That night, lying in her bunk bed, Mackenzie couldn't stop thinking about it. Hollywood was no different than any other money-making industry. People would sell their souls and betray their friends to get a director position at a mid-level tech company; of course, they'd do the same in Hollywood, where there was even more money to be made.

It was sickening. Mackenzie good at sales – no, *great* at sales. She hit her numbers every year and, for the last three years, she'd exceeded them. She was in the top two percent of reps at her company, slated to follow in Steve's footsteps – if she wanted to.

Those things had mattered to her a few months ago, but now? All she wanted to do was brew tea and stare at the ocean. Maybe she was depressed. Or maybe she was grieving Steve and all the lies she'd believed about her future.

Or maybe she'd been chasing the wrong things all her life and confronting them at once put her into this state.

In any case, she had over a hundred unused days off, and Steve was so terrified she'd tell everyone about them that not only was she not getting fired, she hadn't heard a single complaint about her going missing.

She rolled over and closed her eyes. There was a long week of learning about matcha and scanning the water for seals ahead of her.

. . .

Cora left the island for a job interview and didn't make it back in time to help with the tea party. She was devastated, but she insisted on coming the day after in case "any stars are still hanging around."

Russell had finally found the right team to build the sea pen, and he wanted to get everyone together to finalize plans for the last stretch.

He posted about the meetup on the Lottie section of his website and invited friends to stop by. He'd meant people who had donated or had some genuine interest, but it instead led to a slew of talentless hangers-on trying to elbow into the project for publicity.

With her new theory on workplaces, Mackenzie saw it coming a mile away. It was fascinating to watch in real time. Four musicians she'd vaguely heard of offered to come, but never showed up. One B-list movie star made a big show about flying out, took one picture on the island (nowhere near the tea shop), then left.

As they prepared the tea shop on Saturday morning, Granny buzzed around barking orders and trying to guess where everyone would want to sit.

"Do you think Idris Elba would prefer to be in the London or Japanese tearoom?"

Eliza had warned her about Granny's celebrity crush, but it still caught her off guard. She'd never seen Granny so thrilled in her life.

"Granny," Eliza said gently. "I don't think he's coming. He's married, you know. Plus, you have Reggie. You're not free to flirt with Idris."

"This isn't about flirting! Maybe I just want to meet him, Did you ever think of that? Maybe we'd get along!"

Reggie piped up from his seat, a half-folded napkin in his hand. "Hey! I'm not letting that guy in here!"

"Oh yes you are!" Granny said. "I will not let your petty jealousies get in the way of meeting one of the loveliest gentlemen of our time!"

Reggie laughed. "*Our* time, eh?"

She stopped, glaring at him, and he lowered his head.

"I didn't invite him," Russell said, walking in with a box in his arms, "because I couldn't stand to see a rift between you and Reg."

"One of these days, Russell," Granny muttered, walking away, "I will get you back for this."

He turned to look at Mackenzie and Eliza. "Was that a threat?"

Mackenzie nodded. "Just about."

Starting at ten, Joey flew in planeloads of contractors, Lottie's veterinarians, and low-level celebrities to the island. Others arrived by private jet, and Russell rode to the airport to pick up truckload after truckload of Hollywood's elite.

Mackenzie had no preference for what her task was in this tea party and ended up washing the floors twice at Granny's urging. Eliza prepared the plates of sweets and by noon, the tea shop was full of bodies.

"Is Joey going to be able to join us today?" Mom asked Russell. "Or are you working him to death?"

"He should be able to take a break soon," Russell said, looking at his watch. "I want to make sure he has some time to enjoy the company."

He winked at Eliza. She blinked once, then turned and walked into the kitchen.

"Yikes." Russell winced. "Was it something I said?"

"I'll talk to her. Don't worry," Mackenzie said, pushing the kitchen door open. "What was that about?" she asked.

Eliza didn't turn around, intently focused on measuring loose tea. "Nothing."

"Are you too busy to see Joey?"

No response.

"Did something happen between you two?"

"There's nothing between us," she said, then quickly spun around. "Why? Did he say something to you?"

Mackenzie shook her head. "I haven't talked to him."

"Oh." She turned back to the tea.

"Eliza. You're being weird. What happened?"

She shrugged, resuming her apparent vow of silence.

Mackenzie sighed. "I know I'm not always the best person to talk to, but I'm trying to be better. I'm not trying to judge you or tell you what to do."

"It's not you," Eliza said. "I like talking to you."

"Then talk!"

She wiped her hands on her apron and let out a heavy sigh. "You're going to have a hard time not judging me."

"No, please!" Mackenzie put her hands up. "I'm different now. I mean, I'm trying to be different. I want to help. What's going on?"

Eliza studied her for a moment before motioning for her to come closer. She reached into her pocket and pulled out a small leather tassel.

Mackenzie reached forward. "What is that?"

"It's a tassel from a cowboy hat."

She waved it. "Is it yours?"

"No. It's from the hat the bank robber wore."

Mackenzie's mouth dropped open. "You found it?"

"I did." She cleared her throat. "In the back of Joey's plane."

Twenty

Mackenzie's brow furrowed. She opened her mouth to speak, but quickly shut it. Then she gasped.

Eliza watched her face carefully, and with every passing emotion, the lead balloon on her chest lifted higher and higher.

"Wait." Mackenzie handed the tassel back. "Does this mean what I think it means?"

Eliza tucked it into her pocket and dropped her voice to a whisper. "At the very least, it means he's been lying to me."

"Do you think he's...?" She paused. "You know. *Him?*"

The room lurched beneath her and bile pooled at the back of her throat.

Steady. No throwing up in the tea shop. "Maybe."

Mackenzie gasped. "And if he is? What's he going to do to you when he knows you've figured it out?"

"That's what I've been wondering myself."

"Did you tell the police yet? Or whoever came to the bank – the FBI?"

"The ATF," Eliza corrected. "I hadn't gotten there yet. I went back to the bank in town. The manager was really nice and helped me apply for a loan, but she didn't remember anything new. Then at the coffee shop, I saw Stacy, the ATF agent who was mean to me."

Mackenzie winced. "Aw, man. You don't want to tell her. She'll be mean to you again."

"No. I didn't *see* her, exactly. Wally showed me a video of her throwing the wheelchair from the robbery into the coffee shop dumpster."

Mackenzie's mouth popped open. "What? Why? *What* is going on? That was evidence, wasn't it?"

She nodded. "As far as I know, yes."

"Why would she throw it away?"

"I have no idea. I've been trying to figure it out all week, and I'm not sure where else to look."

Eliza rubbed her face with her hands. Her eyelids were swollen and heavy. She'd been up late trying to find out more about Joey, but to no avail. Aside from pictures of his fabulous travels, his online presence was void of any substance.

"I'm scared of Stacy and I can't find anything about Joey that would make this make sense."

Mackenzie bit her lip. "Don't you kind of want to ask him and see what he says?"

"So he can get spooked and fly away?" She shook her head. "No way."

"Hm. Good point." Mackenzie leaned back against the kitchen counter. "They could be working together, somehow. Him and Stacy."

Leave it to Mackenzie to suspect a secret liaison.

But she wasn't wrong. Eliza shut her eyes. "It's possible."

"Or maybe...it's something more than that? Something romantic?"

She slowly breathed out, distancing herself from the sting. "It's crossed my mind."

Mackenzie crossed her arms over her chest. "Stacy's got to be in on it. Are you sure the bank robber was a man?"

Eliza nodded. "That, at least, I'm sure of."

"Okay." She nodded. "Wait, I just remembered! When you went to look for that truck, she just happened to be there."

Her stomach lurched at the memory of Joey greeting her then. Were they partners in crime? Partners in *love*? All this time, she hadn't a clue...

She brushed the thought away. "I guess...I don't know. This is going to sound crazy."

"Hit me with it," Mackenzie said, a grin on her face. "I'm just a sounding board, remember?"

Eliza smiled back at her. Mack was doing well with this whole non-judgmental thing and Eliza did feel better, even if they were coming to the same exact conclusions. "What if he's the robber and he thought I might be able to recognize him, so he tried to, you know, seduce me so I'd fall in love with him. After he met Stacy, he thought she was onto him, so he seduced her, too."

She scrunched up her nose. "I'll be honest, that's a lot of seducing. I don't know that Joey has it in him."

Eliza laughed. "I'm just brainstorming."

She put up a hand. "Nothing surprises me anymore. Maybe he didn't seduce her, just offered her some of the money he's stolen. He's gotten millions at this point, right?"

"I guess. Yeah."

"Or he could've just offered her a ride for the right price."

The idea that perhaps Eliza had been the only one he'd tried to charm romantically lifted her spirits for a moment, but she quickly swatted them down.

It was absurd. He was probably a criminal. Any feelings he'd had toward her were fake. She was nothing more than a tool to him.

A chill ran down her spine and her shoulders quivered.

Mackenzie reached out to touch her hand. "You don't look so good. Why don't you go back to the cottage and take a nap?"

"I'm okay."

"I insist. I'll cover for you here and, afterwards, we'll make a plan. I can find out more about Stacy."

She shook her head. "We can't go digging for stuff on her. Won't she know if we look her up? She's a special agent."

Mackenzie scoffed. "You watch too many movies. No, don't worry—we do this all the time in sales. We spy on our customers. Well, not spy, but get an idea of who they are using creative techniques."

"Ah."

Eliza was only half listening. What was Joey doing right now? Laughing at how dumb she'd been, how easy she was to trick?

"Go on. Take a nap, then we'll reconvene."

The suggestion of sleep made her head feel even heavier. She yawned. "Are you sure?"

"I am." Mackenzie tugged at the strings on Eliza's apron and pushed her toward the door. "We'll figure this out. I'm glad you told me."

She smiled. "Me too."

. . .

Back in her room, Eliza took off her glasses and slipped under the covers. The sheets were cool and soft and within seconds, she was out.

The next time she opened her eyes was to darkness. She sat up, grabbing her glasses and trying to remember what day it was.

"Hey," Mackenzie called out from the bottom bunk.

Eliza climbed down. Mackenzie was sitting on her bed, her face lit by the glow of a laptop.

"I found the business card you got from Stacy and dug up some information about her."

She pulled a sweatshirt on and sat next to her. "Are you sure she's not going to get a notification you're investigating her?"

"I doubt it." She clicked to another screen. "I friended her on Facebook and I can see all of her pictures. It's all just *there*."

"You *friended* her? Are you out of your mind?"

"Relax. It's not me; it's one of the fake profiles we use at work to investigate people."

Eliza frowned. "You work at a weird place."

"Tell me about it." She clicked through Stacy's pictures one by one. "She fell for our 'handsome man' profile pretty fast."

Interesting. Eliza had fallen for a handsome man once. "Any pictures of her with Joey?"

"No."

Eliza breathed out. "He's not online much anyway."

"My first thought was that maybe she's not a real ATF agent, but she is. I confirmed it. She used to work at the DEA before this."

She clicked to a picture of Stacy standing on a picnic table and shotgunning a beer.

"Oh my," Eliza said. "I didn't take her as a party girl."

"Yeah. She's only a few years older than me." She paused. "That was from the DEA family picnic."

She sputtered a laugh. "That was a work event?"

"Mhm." She tapped through the pictures, stopping on one of Stacy with her arm around a man with salt and pepper hair.

"Is that her dad?" Eliza asked.

"He was her director at the DEA." Mackenzie tilted her head. "I have a theory—she had to leave the DEA because they were having an affair."

"How do you know that?"

She shrugged. "Just a feeling I have. Look how close her face was to his. He's married, you know. At least, he was."

Eliza rolled her eyes. "So you've decided she's a federal employee problem child? You're just making up biases."

"It makes sense, though. Before she was at the DEA, she was teaching marketing part time at the community college."

Eliza frowned. "That is a strange career path, but it doesn't mean anything."

"She started with a degree in criminal justice." Mackenzie tapped her fingers on the keys. "I don't know—she's all over the place. She got expelled from her college dorm during her freshman year."

"Where did you find that?"

"From an article she published in the school paper. She's a terrible writer."

Eliza laughed. "I really feel like you're not an impartial investigator. You just really hate Stacy."

"I'm impartial! But, yes, she was mean to you, and she seems like the least serious federal agent I've ever seen."

"Have you known a lot of them?"

She turned her nose up. "Maybe I have."

"Yeah, okay." Eliza sighed, sitting back. "This is all interesting, but it doesn't prove Stacy is involved."

Or that Joey was innocent.

"I'm going to find something." Mackenzie clicked on a picture of Stacy drinking from a large bottle of champagne – New Years 2019. "I just know it."

Mackenzie's answer came early the next morning when Stacy posted a picture of herself in Anacortes. The caption read, "Living my best life – crab buffet brunch!"

"Get your shoes, come on, come on!" Mackenzie rushed around the room, grabbing bags and coats.

"We can't stalk a special agent!" Eliza said. "She'll put us in jail."

"For what? I like crab. I just want to get some crab."

Eliza buried her face in her hands. "I don't think this is a good idea. And I need to work."

Mackenzie finally stopped moving and looked her in the eye. "It's not the best idea, but you might be in love with a criminal, so we have to do something. Cora came back for a few days and she owes us one. She can cover the shop. Come on!"

Mackenzie had her there.

Eliza groaned. "I'll drive."

Twenty-one

I t was starting to feel like Eliza was avoiding him. Joey had hoped to see her on the day of the tea party, but he'd had so many flights he didn't get a chance to go inside the tea shop until she was long gone.

He'd offered to help clean up, but after half an hour, there was still no sign of her.

"Is Eliza around?" he asked Mackenzie as casually as he could muster.

"She's not feeling well."

"Oh. Can I check on her?"

She shook her head. "I'm sure she's asleep."

After they locked up the shop, he sent Eliza a text. "Sorry to hear you're sick. I'm also sorry I've been MIA recently – Russell needed me for a lot of flights. I guess I have to do my job occasionally, ha."

She wrote back the next morning. "Ha ha, yeah. I've been busy too. Maybe we'll find some time next week?"

He first wrote out, "I'd love that," decided it was too eager, and instead sent, "Sure!"

He spent the rest of the evening in an unfamiliar state – racking his brain for what he might've done to offend her.

This was uncharted territory. He rarely stayed in one place long enough to develop any sort of relationship, let alone one that made him doubt himself.

Was it Cora? Had she told Eliza what they talked about and now she was too embarrassed to face him?

His stomach churned at the thought. If only he could ease her mind and put into words the strange pull he had toward her, while simultaneously assuring her it was nothing to worry about.

Every time he tried to think it through, his body became unbearably fidgety. His shoulders ached, his scalp itched, and the muscles in his legs cramped. The longer he went without seeing her, the more he thought about her, until there was little else he could think of.

Joey took a late walk that evening and scanned the dark sky, tracing the stars above. He walked and walked, venturing further, then closer to shore, the sound of the water crashing fading and building as he powered on.

He returned to the house only when his legs were tired and his face was frozen from the wind.

On Monday morning, Russell ruined his plans to stick around the tea shop all day.

"Bad news. All the morning ferries coming in from Anacortes were canceled."

Joey groaned. "Again?"

"Yep. I've got some workers on the way with supplies. We'll have to leave some things behind, but can you pick them up?"

It wasn't like the walking had solved anything. Maybe a delay in going to the tea shop was a good thing. It would give him more time to think. "Sure."

He landed in Anacortes and taxied as close as he could near the ferry terminal. A wall of cars and trucks were stacked upon the sea, sunlight glistening from the clear blue water and onto the scowling faces of stranded passengers.

He tied the plane up and walked down the dock. Children splashed in the shallow waters, shrieking and giggling. The adults' faces were without smiles, sullen and red.

His phone rang. Russell.

"Hey, I just heard they hired a water taxi."

"Oh." He stopped walking. "Okay. I just got here. Is there anyone else I should pick up?"

"Not that I know of. Maybe later? We'll see. Sorry to waste a flight."

A couple came down the steps from the commissary with ice creams in hand.

Now there was an idea for a good breakfast.

"Not wasted. I'll get something to eat. Do you want anything?"

"I'm good. Thanks, Joey!"

Maybe there was some tea on the mainland he could buy for Eliza? It'd be a great excuse to see her.

The ferry terminal was a bit far from town, but he could try walking. Or hitchhiking. Except for the bank robberies, it was an incredibly safe place to live. What were the chances he'd run into that guy again anyway?

He was staring at the map on his phone when he felt a tap on his shoulder. Joey looked up and saw a set of bright white teeth. "Hey there, is that your plane?"

Joey looked over his shoulder. "Uh, yes."

"Is there any way I can get a ride to Orcas Island? There might not be a ferry for hours and I've really got to get over there."

Something about her voice was familiar. He stared at her dark, shining hair, and the big, black sunglasses perched on her small nose.

Agent Stacy. Now *there* was something Eliza would want to hear about. If he could get her to say anything...

"You're with ATF, aren't you?"

She raised her eyebrows. "I am. Have we met?"

"Briefly," he said with a laugh. "You're investigating the robbery."

"That's right!" Her expression brightened. "I need to get to the island to look into some things."

"I'd be happy to give you a lift." They walked outside, the sun burning a hole in the bright blue sky. "As long as you tell me more about the case."

She laughed. "Right. I'll tell you...and every other nosy busy body."

He wasn't going to give up that easily. Joey smiled at her, leading the way down the dock and toward the plane.

Twenty-two

"He's holding her hand! *Look!*" Mackenzie jabbed her finger in the air.

Eliza had lost all fear of Stacy seeing her. She stood, hands on the dock railing, staring at Joey. Her heart sank. Maybe it wasn't what they thought. Maybe...

"He always helps me onto the plane, too," she said weakly.

"That snake!" Mackenzie hissed. "Who does he think he is, playing you like that!"

A breeze blew off the ocean as Eliza flopped onto a bench. The hard wood jolted her tailbone.

"I'm going to confront him," Mackenzie said.

"Don't." Eliza grabbed her by the wrist. "There's no use."

"Catching him in the act? I beg to differ."

Eliza stared straight ahead. Joey and Stacy were inside the plane now, the propeller spinning and the engine sputtering. It was odd hearing it from so far away, buzzing like that. She was used to it filling her ears, the vibration shaking her chest as Joey's voice cracked over her headphones.

"You're right," Mackenzie said, stepping closer. "It's better if we report them to someone. Maybe the FBI? If Stacy is a crooked agent—"

Eliza cut her off. "I'm not ready to go to the FBI."

She crossed her arms. "Why not?"

It was a cool day, but somehow the air felt thick and heavy. The heat from the sun was oppressive.

Eliza coughed and rubbed her face with her hands. "It doesn't make sense."

"It does make sense if you consider he's a liar."

The plane lifted from the water and gracefully rose into the sky. Eliza sat back. "He doesn't seem like a criminal."

"They never do."

Eliza scrunched her nose. Her sister was a bit too riled up over this. Almost as though she was projecting.

Not that she was going to say that to her. "Stacy does seem like a criminal – a dumb one."

But not Joey...

Mackenzie nodded and pointed at her. "Here's the thing. We're used to hearing about the dumb criminals because they're the ones who get caught. The good ones blend in and fly planes and charm even the smartest of people."

Fly planes. Ha.

Eliza winced, looking down at her feet. She was wearing her favorite sneakers, a pair of black and white Adidas Sambas.

She'd gotten them for her birthday two years ago and, determined to keep them neat and clean, hardly ever wore them.

There was mud caked on the front of her right shoe from her most recent outing with Joey. She had liked the way the shoes had made her feel that day. She liked the way Joey made her feel every day.

"I'm sorry, Eliza. I know you liked him." Mackenzie softened her tone. "But I speak from experience. Loving someone isn't enough. It won't make them love you back, especially when they suck."

She stood. "I think we should go back home."

Mackenzie didn't push. "Okay."

. . .

Getting back to the island was easier said than done. With the ferry cancellations, they got bumped further and further into the day. They had to leave their car in line at the terminal, and there wasn't much to do there.

They walked the entirety of the shoreline, first separately, then together, carefully skirting around any sore subjects when they spoke. They finally made the ferry after sunset and got back to the tea shop as Cora was cleaning up.

"Your granny is not happy with me," Cora said. "She told me to clean up the unsold pastries for the day. I put them in the trash and—"

"Cora!" Mackenzie snapped. "Did they look like trash to you?"

It'd be best to separate them for now. Eliza stepped in. "It's okay. Not a big deal. Thanks for covering today."

"You're welcome." She let out a heavy sigh and took a seat at a nearby table. "I'll be honest—it was rough. I don't think I'm cut out for shop life, and no one from Hollywood is taking the bait, either."

"You'll figure something out," Eliza said, patting her on the shoulder.

"Yeah." She shrugged. "How was your day stalking Stacy?"

"We found her," Eliza said.

"Anything suspicious to report?" Cora asked.

Mackenzie was staring at her. She didn't want to say it. She never wanted to speak of it again if at all possible.

Mackenzie cleared her throat. "Joey picked her up. In the seaplane."

Cora gasped. "Wait, I forgot. He came looking for you!"

Eliza's head shot up. "He did?"

"Eliza," Mackenzie said slowly. "I think maybe you shouldn't talk to him anymore."

Cora went on. "He seemed distressed. I probably shouldn't tell you this, but he asked if you were avoiding him."

Her heart, the poor thing, leapt in her chest.

"He must know we're catching on to him," Mackenzie said. "Typical scammer, trying to cover his tracks."

Cora bit her lip. "I'm not sure that's it. I might've let something slip that I shouldn't have."

Daggers could've shot out of Mackenzie's eyes and hit Cora like a bullseye. "You told him we suspected him? You're going to put us all in danger!"

Cora rolled her eyes. "No one is in danger. It was nothing to do with the robbery."

"What was it?" Eliza asked.

She shifted her weight. "Don't get mad at me, Eliza, but I might have hinted that you like him." She stopped, then rushed to add, "It's not a big deal."

Eliza couldn't help it. A smile crept onto her face. "And he seemed intrigued?"

"Very. He's interesting, though," she said, tapping her chin. "He told me he fell in love once and acted like he's never going to fall in love again."

Eliza's heart tightened in her chest. "Oh. So he doesn't feel anything for me."

"I didn't say that." Cora shook her head. "If he's so cool and unaffected, why did he care so much about finding you?"

"He only wants to know if you're going to turn him in," Mackenzie said. "Eliza, you can't fall for this."

Her heart was in her throat. "Did he say anything else?"

"Not really. He asked me to let you know he was sorry he couldn't catch you today."

"*Catch* you," Mackenzie repeated. "Do you think that means something?"

Eliza didn't know what it meant, but she knew what she hoped it meant and there went her stomach, flipping and turning.

His voice popped into his head. What was it he'd said at game night to Mackenzie? *Next time, leave before you're left.*

The words knocked her heart back into her chest. She'd thought he was joking or was trying to make Mackenzie feel better.

But now, as sudden as a canceled ferry, she knew he'd meant it. Really meant it.

Joey had never made any promises to her. Sure, he didn't come out and say he wasn't the robber, but he had also never given her a reason to believe he was interested in anything but himself. He had either been pretending to look for the robber, knowing full well he was the one, or he was peripherally involved. No matter what, he was honest about his plan to get as much cash as he could for a plane and then fly off.

She knew who he was, robber or not. He was exactly who he'd presented himself to be: a guy who had no plans to stick around.

"Excuse me," she said, escaping into the bathroom.

She flicked on the light and shut herself inside. Thankfully, none of their British customers had yet complained about Granny's attempt at a themed bathroom. The red walls, the black and white picture of Big Ben, the random British flag above the toilet – none of it was comforting in her current state, and she couldn't imagine anyone genuinely liked it.

Eliza went to the sink and turned on the cold water, splashing it on her face. It eased some of the hot feeling rushing to her cheeks. She stood, savoring it for a moment, before turning to get a paper towel.

She bumped into something with her foot and squatted down. It was a small black duffel bag. Without thinking, she unzipped it and her eyes fell onto a hint of green at the bottom of the bag. She pushed aside the darker items to uncover a stack of one hundred dollar bills.

She gasped. "Mackenzie! Cora!"

"What's wrong?" Mackenzie called back.

"Come here! Now!"

Their footsteps rushed to the bathroom Eliza flung the door open. "What is this doing in here?"

"Oh, money!" Cora said, reaching forward.

Mackenzie slapped her hand. "Stop! You can't just grab piles of random money."

She leaned forward and carefully picked every item out of the bag: a blue surgical mask, a ladies cowboy hat with a colorful leather band, a brick of wrapped hundred dollar bills.

"Is this what I think it is?" Mackenzie asked.

Eliza nodded. "That's the hat from the robbery. And the money..."

Mackenzie stood and backed away. "I'm not going to touch it in case there are ink packs in there or something."

Eliza's head was tingling. She reminded herself to take a breath. "How did this get here?"

"I have no idea!" Cora said. "It was busy today. A lot of people were going in and out."

"It had to be Joey." Mackenzie shook her head. "He came here and dropped this bag off."

Eliza leaned down and stared at the hat. It was just as she remembered it. "Maybe it's his confession? Maybe he wanted me to have it, and to have some of the money?"

"Oh no!" Cora groaned. "That's why he wanted to see you so badly. He wanted to say goodbye."

Tears stung her eyes. She sucked in a breath. "That might be it."

"What do we do with this?" Mackenzie squatted down next to her. "Do we turn it in?"

At least now she knew the truth. That was better than nothing, she supposed.

"I don't know," she said, her voice shaking.

"Oh, don't cry," Cora stooped down, wrapping them both in a hug. "I'm sure there's an explanation."

"Yeah," Eliza said, wiping a tear. "I'm sure there is."

That explanation being *leave before you're left*.

Twenty-three

A new shipment of teacups arrived from Japan, and Patty was the one who got to unpack them.

It was a *wonderful* day.

Thanks to Eliza's ingenuity in reviving the business, Patty got to order beautiful tea sets all the time. Some were sold in the shop, others on the website. Every so often, a set would come in that was too beautiful to part with and she'd add it to her own collection.

Today was extra special because Sheila had decided to work from the tea shop while Patty unpacked. Eliza was still under the weather and Mackenzie was running things in her place.

"I don't know what's going on with her," Sheila said quietly, settling into a table with her laptop and papers.

"Must have caught a bug," Patty said, cutting the tape on the box. She opened it and stopped to admire the tight packaging. Nothing had broken. How lucky she was!

"I don't buy it." Sheila dropped her voice. "I think it has something to do with Joey. Have you seen him around?"

There was a delicate box under the bubble wrap, pink and gold, nested in a mound of pink and white shredded paper. "Why don't you ask Mackenzie?"

Sheila looked up from her laptop. "She won't tell me a thing. If I ask her any questions about Eliza, she changes the subject to the sea pen or my music."

"How is your last song coming along?" Patty asked.

Sheila sighed. "Fine."

"Doesn't sound fine," Patty said with a smile.

She shut her laptop. "You're doing the same thing! Changing the subject!"

"I'm not changing the subject. I'm curious about your progress!" She turned from the box to face Sheila. "Is it Lottie? Are you upset because you haven't been allowed to see her?"

The other owners of Marine Magic Funland had first hit Sheila with a lawsuit. When that went nowhere, they whipped up a restraining order to keep her away from the park.

It was a lot of silliness. Lottie would be living a short boat ride away in a matter of months.

"No, Lottie is doing great. I'm worried about Eliza."

"I think you're right; she's come down with a bug. A *love* bug." Patty laughed. "You remember being young, all the drama. I'm sure she'll tell us when she's ready."

The door to teashop swung open with a jingle. A man and a woman walked in dressed in matching black vests, the letters ATF across their chests in white lettering.

Sheila stood from her seat. "Hi. Can I help you?"

"I'm Special Agent Grouper and this is my partner, Special Agent Wallace," the woman said. "We need to talk to Eliza Dennet."

Patty stared at the agent. She was short and slim, with hard eyes and a pair of large sunglasses sitting atop her head. "Are you the agent who talked to Eliza after the robbery?"

She nodded. "Is she here?"

Mackenzie emerged from the kitchen. "What's going on?"

Patty set down the box with the carefully packed pair of teacups.

This was the woman who'd accused her granddaughter of robbing a bank? The one who had called her stupid?

"Eliza isn't here today," Patty said firmly. "Thanks for your inquiry."

"If it's all right with you, we'd like to have a look around," agent Wallace said. "We received a tip—"

"I don't care what you received," Patty said, hands on her hips. "Unless you have a warrant, there will be no looking around."

The lady agent scoffed. "Ma'am, we're trying to help."

Sheila's eyes darted between them. "I'm sure we can—"

"We don't need any help from you," Patty said with a nod. "Thank you. Goodbye."

The lady agent put her hands on her hips. One of her hands rested near a handgun hanging in a holster. "I need to use the bathroom before I go."

"Of course, go ahead," Sheila said before Patty could say no.

Mackenzie leapt forward. "I'll show you where it is."

Patty stood, arms crossed, staring down the other agent.

He walked to the counter, eyeing their display of tea sets and loose-leaf tea. "You have a lovely shop."

"I know." Patty lifted her chin, her stare unbroken.

"May I?" He picked up a tin of tea from the front counter. "I'd love this for my mom."

Patty narrowed her eyes. "All right."

She walked to the register and he handed her a fifty dollar bill.

"You expect me to break this for you?" Patty sighed.

He flashed a half smile. "I'm sorry. It's all I've got."

She let out another sigh, rung him up, and handed him his change.

"I don't need a bag." He winked at her. "Have a nice day."

The lady agent returned a moment later, walking past her partner without stopping. "Let's go."

He nodded goodbye, and the two of them left through the front door. Patty watched through the window as they got into their car and drove off. She locked the front door and turned back to face Sheila and Mackenzie.

"Patty! Why were you so rude to them?" Sheila said.

"Because they were looking for our Eliza! And not for a good reason."

"You don't know that. Maybe there was a development in the case."

"I am no stranger to law enforcement. Chief Hank is one of my favorite people on the island. But that was *not* a friendly visit," Patty said firmly. She picked up the lovely teacup set and gently nestled it back into its box. Today was not the day for lovely things.

"She didn't use the bathroom," Mackenzie said. "She went in, flushed, and walked right back out."

Sheila tilted her head to the side. "You were watching her? What has gotten into you two?"

Mackenzie nodded. "That was Stacy. She's the agent who was mean to Eliza."

"Oh. *Oh.*" Sheila's lips hardened into a line. "I'm glad you were rude to her, then."

"She was looking for something," Mackenzie said. "A bag."

"What bag?" Patty asked.

Mackenzie bit her lip. "You're both going to be...unhappy with me."

"Mack, honey," Sheila said, "if something is going on, you need to tell us."

She pulled out a chair, scraping it against the hardwood floor. "Long story short, we think Joey robbed the bank and that Stacy is in on it. They're dating, maybe. And he hid a bag with the robbery disguise and a bunch of money in the bathroom last night."

"What!" Sheila shouted. "Why didn't you tell me any of this?"

"It's Eliza," Mackenzie sighed. "She's convinced he's not involved and she doesn't want to tell anyone yet."

Sheila covered her eyes with hand. "She's protecting him."

"She's sick," Patty said. "Heartsick. It's a terrible disease. Infects every system."

"Not funny, Patty." Sheila glared at her. "This is serious!"

"Why did they want to talk to Eliza?" Patty peered out the window. "That Stacy was so forceful."

"We thought maybe Joey had left her the money as an apology," Mackenzie said. "But maybe they were trying to frame her?"

"Why don't we ask him?" Patty said, peering through the window. "He's headed right for the door."

"Get down!" Mackenzie barked. "Now!"

Sheila and Mackenzie squatted quickly. Patty had a harder time moving quickly.

"I can't get down with such short notice," she complained, grabbing a chair with one hand and lowering herself. "I need more time."

"Lower, Granny!" Mackenzie whispered, reaching for her arm.

Patty felt herself starting to fall backwards, so she stood back up. "I can't do it!"

"Just sit down, then!" Sheila whispered.

Patty eased into a seat, then slumped over. "There. Is that good?"

The door rattled, once, twice, as Joey pulled at the knob.

"Hello?" he called out. His face appeared in the window.

Patty sunk lower. "I think he can see me."

"Sh!"

His face disappeared. Patty's back hurt too much to sit like this. She stood and looked through the window. Joey was walking down the hill.

"That's it." Patty dusted off her apron. "I'm not going to hide on the floor in my own teashop. We're going to get help."

"Who?" Sheila asked, standing up.

Patty smiled. "Let's just say I have connections."

"Chief Hank?" Sheila asked.

"Better. His wife, Margie."

Mackenzie frowned. "How is Margie going to help with this?"

Patty dropped her apron on the chair. "Just – come with me."

Sheila and Mackenzie shot each other a look.

"Trust me! I'm older than both of you combined, and more than twice as wise," she said. "Get your coats; it looks like rain."

Finally, they did as she said and followed her out the door.

Twenty-four

There was no use pretending. Eliza was avoiding him, and everyone else was, too.

Joey had heard them whispering inside the tea shop, and when he peeked through the smudged glass, he saw Eliza's Granny trying to hide from him, contorting herself in a chair.

He was unwanted. He didn't know why, but it was time to take the hint.

The air was cool and the wind cut through his jacket as he walked back to Russell's house. When he reached the thicket of trees between the properties, he turned to look back at the cottage. It was dark except for a single glowing window upstairs.

Joey pulled out his phone and called.

Eliza picked up mid-ring. "Joey?"

Her voice bounced in his ear, soft and strong. "Hey, yeah, hi."

Eliza cleared her throat. "Is everything okay?"

He looked up. Above him, half of the sky was black with clouds, and the other half glowed an eerie orange. The light filtered through the tangled branches of trees, casting webs of shadows around him. "I think we need to talk."

She was quiet. The wind rattled the empty branches above. "Okay. Where are you?"

"I was just walking back from the tea shop. Are you there?"

"No." Quiet for a moment. "I can meet you down at the beach, though."

His heart leapt. "Okay. I'll see you in a minute."

The wind blew against him and he nearly tripped, first over the twisted roots of the trees, then rushing across the beach with the unexpected sinking of his shoes into the dry stones.

A hooded figure emerged from the cottage and grew larger, closing in. A flash of light cracked above him. He saw Eliza's face rimmed with black fleece.

"Hi," she said when she reached him. "Looks like it's going to storm."

"Yeah." He didn't care. His heart raced. "Are you okay? I haven't heard from you in so long."

A smile flicked at the corner of her mouth. "I'm fine. Are you okay?"

"Yeah." He paused. What was the point of dragging her out here if he wasn't going to tell the truth? "I really miss you."

She looked down. "I saw you yesterday. In Anacortes."

He smiled. "Really? I didn't see you. Where were you?"

She looked up, locking eyes with him. "I saw you with Stacy."

He looked up, the last scraps of light overtaken with clouds. "Oh, yeah. Russell sent me to pick up some people, but they found another way to the site. She came up to me and said she needed a ride."

She peered up at him. "Did she."

"I tried to get something out of her," he continued, "but she wouldn't say a word. Steel trap."

Eliza pulled her jacket tight over her chest. "Is that the truth, Joey?"

He focused his gaze on her. "Yes. You'd be the first person to know if she told me anything useful."

"No. I mean about everything." Her voice softened. "I'm not going to turn you in, you know."

Waves pulsed closer, one nearly hitting his shoes. "What? Turn me in?"

"Why did you want to work with me, Joey? Why did you want me to help you find the robber?"

His chest tightened and his guts twisted. She knew. He didn't know how, but she did.

He took a deep breath. "There are two parts to this."

Eliza's expression didn't change, her eyes slowly scanning his face, left to right, up and down. She tilted her head as if to get another angle.

He went on. "First of all, Granny offered me twenty-five dollars to scare off the kids who were trying to torment you."

She frowned. "She never told me that."

"Ask her." He cracked a smile. "Well, actually, ask her for the last five dollars, because she only gave me twenty."

"What's the second part?"

He wanted to say it. He did. It was on the edge of his throat, but he kept biting it back, the words too harsh and acrid. "Because...I thought you'd be the best person to find the bank robber. That's the truth."

She kept her eyes on him, waiting for more. When he didn't add anything, she said, "What about the bag in the tea shop?"

He scrunched his eyebrows. "What bag?"

"Don't lie to me, Joey. Please."

"I don't know about a bag. The robbery bag?"

She shrugged. "I don't know if it was the robbery bag." She paused. "But I know you were involved in it."

He shut his eyes, the shame crashing in. "How did you figure it out?"

"Just lucky, I guess."

Joey ran a hand through his hair. "It's embarrassing."

"More embarrassing than carrying a bomb into a bank?"

A drop of water hit him in the cheek. He looked up. "You'll think I'm an idiot."

"Try me."

He sucked in a breath. The air cut his lungs but he held it, trying to get the first words out. "The morning of the robbery, Russell had me flying a bunch of people around. It was my second week here.

"A guy showed up. Black bag over his shoulder, cowboy hat. He had a big mustache, but I don't remember much else. Friendly guy. Asked me for a ride back to Anacortes, saying he was supposed to pick something up for Russell."

"He had a cowboy hat?"

Joey nodded. "I didn't think anything of it. I really didn't, until I saw the police sketch of the guy in the hat."

Eliza was silent, biting the inside of her cheek. "You didn't think to tell me this before?"

"I didn't want..." His voice trailed off. "I couldn't pick him out of a lineup if you offered me a million dollars. I wasn't even sure he wasn't one of Russell's guys until you told me about the hat. Then I was sure."

"And you *still* didn't tell me?"

He dropped his shoulders. "I'm really sorry. I didn't want you to think I was part of it."

"Well, yeah." She let out a breath and drew herself up. "I found the tassel in your plane."

"Oh." Misting rain coated his face. He squinted. "You already knew."

She sniffed, touching her reddened nose with the back of her hand. "I didn't know for sure. Mackenzie's convinced you're the robber."

"What?" A gust of salted air blew into his eyes. "I'm not the robber!"

"How can I be sure?"

The wind wouldn't let up. He jerked his head, trying to keep it out of his eyes. "Is that why you've been avoiding me? You really think I've been robbing banks and forgot to tell you?"

Her phone buzzed and she pulled it from her pocket. The screen lit her face for a moment as she typed a message.

Waves crashed into the shore, foaming the smooth rocks. Thunder rumbled in the distance.

She tucked the phone back into her pocket. "What I think is that either way, you're going to leave, so it doesn't matter."

"It doesn't *matter* if I'm the robber?" A swell built in his chest. His breathing picked up. "Are you hearing yourself right now?"

"Either you are the robber and you're going to fly off with your bag of money. Or you're not and we'll find him, then you'll fly off with your bag of money."

"So that's what you think of me?" He was shouting now, over the wind, over his anger. "That I'm just a guy flying away with a bag of money?"

"I don't mean it like that."

She stepped forward, her arm outstretched, as he stepped back.

"What can you possibly mean, then? You think I'm a bank robber, Eliza. You think I'm the lowest of the low, that I've been using you."

"No! I'm saying I can't even think straight because I know you're going to leave."

"Yeah, sure." He shoved his hands into his coat pockets. His fingertips were ice against the smooth lining. "If you didn't want me to leave, then why did you cut me out of everything?"

She turned her head toward the cottage. Joey stopped to listen. A voice rode the wind like a whisper, calling her name.

"You'd better go," he said. "Wouldn't want anyone to think I was stealing from you."

Her mouth fell open. "Joey."

He spun on his heel and started walking, each footstep heavy in the rocks.

When he reached the twist of trees, he turned around. Eliza was gone. There was nothing but the strip of beach in front of him, the downpour blending the horizon with the darkened sea.

Twenty-five

Granny first tried to herd them into her car, but Mackenzie insisted on getting Eliza.

She ran up the stairs in the cottage, shouting. "Eliza! We need to talk!"

No response. She flung open the doors to their room, then the bathroom. Silence except for the rumbling of the incoming storm.

She thundered down the stairs. "She's gone! Missing! Kidnapped, maybe!"

"There's no need to work yourself in a tizzy," Granny said, slowly removing her coat. "Why don't you use that phone you're always staring at and call her?"

"If I call her, she'll think someone died. It's not that dire." She pulled out her phone and sent a text.

Where are you?

The response came back in seconds.

I went for a walk on the beach.

A cool pulse spread over Mackenzie's chest. So she hadn't been arrested or kidnapped, at least not yet.

I need to talk to you, please.

She waited a minute. Two. No response.

Rude.

"Maybe we shouldn't drive in this storm." Granny turned from the window. "I'll just call Margie."

"I'm going to find Eliza." She trotted through the open door, rain blowing in. "Eliza! E-*liz*-a!"

What were the chances Stacy was still sniffing around, looking for her? She pulled the hood of her jacket over her head and pressed on.

The hill sloped down to the water, and Eliza stood like an apparition, her skin milky white, her lips pale and tight.

The wind blew Mackenzie's hood down as she ran to her. "Are you okay?"

She nodded. "I'm fine. What's going on?"

"Stacy came looking for you at the tea shop. Granny sent her away." She looked over her shoulder. There was nothing but the ocean, white-capped and angry. "I think she was looking for the bag. I think she might've tried to plant it on you."

Eliza looked up. "It's raining."

"Uh yeah." She stepped closer. "We should probably throw the bag into the ocean. Get it out of here."

Her gaze floated back down to Mackenzie, her eyes unfocused. "It'll just wash up on shore."

"I was joking." She nodded toward the house. "Granny said she knows someone who can help. Do you want to go talk to them?"

She hesitated, then nodded, and Mackenzie led the way back to the cottage.

Inside, they shut the door and peeled off their coats. Mackenzie's skin radiated heat. At least they were safe in here.

"Girls!"

They walked into the kitchen. Mom and Granny were seated at the table, Granny's cell phone laying face-up.

"I've got Margie on the line," Granny yelled a bit too loud. "She's my friend – I told you about her. Her husband is Chief Hank."

"Hello, ladies!" Margie's voice was clear on the speaker-phone, but Granny fussed with the phone, making it even louder. "Patty just filled me in. Nasty business, isn't it? I didn't like this robbery from the moment I heard about it."

Mom smiled. "Really? Because we all just loved it."

A laugh cackled out of the phone. "I'm going to call my brother, Mike. He retired from the FBI, but he still has contacts. He can help."

Mackenzie raised an eyebrow. She hadn't expected Granny to have FBI friends. She thought it was going to be someone at the library. She took a seat. Eliza hovered next to her.

A quieter voice said something indiscernible on the phone.

"Oh, that's my daughter," Margie said. "She's going to help me do a three-way call. Hang on to your hats!"

Mackenzie pretended to put an invisible hat on her head and made a face at Eliza. She offered a weak smile.

The line went quiet for a minute before returning. "You still there?"

"I'm here," a man's voice said.

Granny leaned in. "We're here, too."

"I did it!" Margie shrieked. "Okay, Mike, say hello."

"Who's gotten themselves into trouble now?" Mike asked.

Mackenzie leaned forward. "My sister is being framed for a robbery she didn't commit."

"Margie said something about a crooked agent?"

"That's what we *think* might be going on," Mackenzie said. "She was mean to Eliza when she was interrogating her and called her stupid."

"That's not exactly what happened," Eliza said quietly. "She asked me if I was stupid."

"That's not the most compelling evidence that she's a crooked agent," Mike said with a laugh. "But go on."

"Eliza found the truck used in the robbery, and the agent just happened to be there. Wait! Then she saw a video of the agent throwing away evidence from the robbery. A wheelchair!"

"Okay, slow down," Mike said. "Throwing evidence away?"

"Into a dumpster," Eliza said.

Mom looked up, her forehead creased. "Why didn't you tell me any of this?"

Eliza looked down and shrugged.

Mackenzie kept talking. "So we followed her, and maybe she saw us, because that night we found a bag stashed at our tea shop with a bunch of stuff from the robbery. Like the disguise and some money."

"Oh. This is getting interesting," Mike said.

"The next morning, she came to the shop and the first thing she did was insist on going into the bathroom."

"Uh, so...she had to go to the bathroom?" Mike asked. "How is that relevant?"

"That's where the bag was left," Eliza clarified.

"She was quite pushy," Granny yelled. "I asked her to leave, but she insisted on going to that bathroom!"

"Huh." Mike grunted. "All right. Is that all you've got?"

"It's a lot!" Mackenzie snapped. "I just didn't tell it in the most coherent way."

He laughed. "I'm not saying it's nothing, but it's a lot of presumption." He was quiet for a moment. "I can see it, but if she's got you in her sights, you might be in trouble."

"Is there someone I can talk to?" Eliza asked. "I'm innocent. Shouldn't it be easy to prove I'm innocent?"

"Unfortunately," Mike said, "innocent people do guilty-looking things sometimes, precisely because they're convinced justice will surely prevail." He sighed. "For now, don't talk to anyone on the case again. I'll put you in touch with a friend at the FBI who can handle this delicately."

"What about Agent Stacy's..." Mackenzie flashed a look at Eliza. "Accomplice? Can we turn him in?"

Eliza looked up at her, glaring.

"Do you have evidence of an accomplice?" Mike asked.

Mackenzie crossed her arms over her chest. If Eliza wasn't willing to turn Joey in because she was in love with him, she'd have to step in. "Not yet. But we will."

"If you're sure you know who it is," Mike said, "Get him to turn her in. That'll solve it quickly."

"We don't know who he is," Eliza said, cutting in.

"I think we might," Mackenzie whispered.

"Whoever he is, he needs to think it's in his best interest to rat her out. Talk to my agent first. She'll figure it out—she's sharp."

Mackenzie looked at Eliza. She had her arms crossed and her gaze was a thousand miles away.

She nudged her with her foot. Eliza looked up.

"Please?" Mackenzie mouthed.

"I'd be happy to talk to her," Eliza said. "Thanks for your help, Mike."

"No problem. I'll send her number over and give her a heads up."

Mackenzie let out a sigh. Mom met her eyes, shaking her head.

"Thanks, Mike! And Margie!" Granny said, waving at the phone. "Toodles! We'll be in touch."

"Toodles," Mackenzie repeated with a smile.

Eliza turned to her. "I'll be the one talking to this agent, okay?"

Mackenzie put her hands up. "Sure! As long as you tell her about the tassel in Joey's plane."

She sat, staring at the table. "I will."

"Good," Mackenzie said.

Mom nodded. "We'll figure this out. Try not to panic."

"We will." Granny stood, a smile on her lips. "I think a nice cup of tea always puts things in perspective. Chamomile, anyone?"

Twenty-six

The storm wiped all the stars from the night sky, leaving an opaque, dusty black. Whenever Eliza caught a blip of light behind a cloud, it disappeared as soon as her eyes focused.

She turned from the window and slipped into bed, her eyelids heavy. After a cup of chamomile from Granny, she'd done as they wanted and called Mike's FBI friend. Her name was Ramona and she'd agreed to meet the next morning in Seattle.

Eliza booked the flight and excused herself, hoping for just a few moments alone to absorb what had happened.

Talking to the FBI seemed drastic, but then all of it felt drastic – the bag full of money, Stacy showing up, Granny chasing Stacy off.

Worst of all, the look on Joey's face when she'd told him how she felt.

She couldn't tell anyone about that, about how his face hardened when she told him what she knew and what she believed. She didn't care if he was the robber. It hadn't come out right, but it was true. No matter what, he was going to leave. That was what she cared about. That was what bothered her the most.

Telling Mackenzie or Granny or Mom about it was impossible. How his face twisted when he backed away from her. How he walked into the storm rather than face her...

In her dreams that night, she ran after him, his dark form disappearing into the rain. A dream lawyer appeared at her door with a message – a box of chocolates and a note. "My client thanks you for your interest."

She woke with a start, her hair soaked and cold.

Eliza got out of bed quietly, peeling off her pajamas before stepping into the shower. She stood under the hot water until her skin turned pink.

Her flight was before sunrise. The strangest part wasn't sneaking out before everyone awoke; it was looking at the pilot's face and not seeing Joey – not his hair, not his nose, not the grin that reached his eyes.

She met with Agent Ramona at a coffee shop. She had round brown eyes, creased at the sides, and purple bags underneath.

She listened to Eliza's story from the beginning, only looking away to write down a line or two.

"My sister is confident Stacy is involved, but I don't know what to think. I just know I wasn't involved and someone's trying to make it look like I am."

Ramona frowned, her sky eyes scanning her notes. "I looked into Stacy. Did you know she used to work for the DEA?"

Eliza nodded. "My sister saw that online."

"Do you know why she left?" She set her pen down and clasped her hands on the table.

Eliza shook her head. "Do you?"

She laughed. "I do, but I can't share it with you."

"Oh, right. Sorry." She smiled, wrapping her hands around her now lukewarm coffee. The barista had offered to sprinkle vanilla into it for her, and she had agreed without thinking. The artificial smell kept sticking in her nose.

"And the bag?" Ramona asked. "The one someone left at the tea shop. Did you bring it?"

It was nice of her to ask, since it was obvious it was sitting beneath them.

Eliza leaned down and pulled it from under her chair. "This is it. Do you think you can get fingerprints from it?"

She shrugged. "Maybe, but probably not."

"I didn't take anything, but I did touch the hat and the ski mask. I did not touch the money."

"You sure about that?" the agent said with a wink.

Eliza looked down, her cheeks flushing red. "I'm sure. We were afraid there might be ink packs in it or something. Also, I knew it was stolen money, and I don't want anything to do with it."

Agent Ramona unzipped the bag and glanced inside. "I'm going to look into this. All of it. If anything else comes up, call me directly, okay?" She slid a small, plain card across the table.

Eliza reached to grab it. The paper stuck to her sweaty palm. "I will. Thank you for your help. You're a lifesaver."

"Happy to be of service. You take care."

. . .

On her return flight to San Juan Island, Eliza had a different pilot who still wasn't Joey. She still couldn't help looking over at him every few minutes, her mind trying to fill in the details to make it him.

It was never him.

They landed and she stepped off the plane onto the dock in Roche Harbor. Her phone dinged with a text and her heart leapt. It could be Joey after all. He could have changed his mind.

She pulled out her phone and stared at the screen.

It was Mackenzie.

Don't come home.

Eliza laughed, writing back, **Why not?**

Her sister's response was a picture of something small and white. Eliza opened it, her smile falling as soon as she saw the black letters at the top: **ARREST WARRANT.**

She scanned, spotting **ELIZABETH DENNET** and the signature of a judge.

Mackenzie texted again. **There was evidence planted in your car.**

"Everything all right? I hope that wasn't too bumpy for you."

Eliza looked up. The not-Joey pilot was speaking to her with his not-Joey face.

She realized her mouth was hanging open. "No, it was wonderful. Thank you."

An *arrest warrant?* Was she supposed to run? Where? Surely they would come looking for her. Was her phone being tracked? Would turning it off work, or could they still find her?

Maybe she watched too many movies. Or maybe, not enough, because clearly—

"Eliza?"

She spun around and her mind went blank. The not-Joey pilot was gone. Her mind had replaced him with a full-sized Joey apparition.

"Joey," she whispered.

He cocked his head to the side. "What are you doing here?"

The sun framed him in her field of view. He hadn't stepped out of her mind. He was really there. She squinted to see him. "I had to take a flight to Seattle."

His eyes softened. "Are you okay?" He stepped closer. "You look really pale."

Without thinking, she handed him her phone, the picture of the arrest warrant still displayed.

He accepted the phone and his eyebrows bunched up.

He was so close. Eliza traced the outline of his cheeks, his nose, and his lips with her eyes...

Joey zoomed in on her name. "This looks real."

"I think it is."

"What are you going to do?" He looked up at her, his mouth a hard line.

"I don't know. I was thinking I should get rid of this phone so they can't track me."

Without a word, he pulled his arm back and chucked her phone into the sea. It disappeared beneath the surface with a small plop.

She covered her mouth. A laugh escaped from her. "What is happening right now? Why are you here?"

"I just flew some guys in from the sea pen site to get lunch in the harbor."

"Have you heard from anyone? Stacy? The FBI?"

He frowned. "No. Why would the FBI talk to me?"

Sunlight reflected off the water onto his face. She stared, memorizing every detail. "I had to talk to them. It's a friend of a friend, nothing official. I had to tell them about the bag at the tea shop."

"The bag," he repeated slowly.

"It had the cowboy hat and a ski mask and a bunch of money in it. I think Stacy is trying to frame me."

His eyebrows shot up. "Wow."

"I had to tell them about you. Nothing but the facts – we were looking together, you're a pilot. You gave her a ride to the island."

"I see." He looked down and sighed. "And me giving the robber a getaway flight?"

"It didn't come up." That was the truth. Ramona hadn't asked and Eliza hadn't offered.

"Ah. I see."

He hadn't left. Not yet at least. He was standing here in front of her, weighing his options.

"I didn't think I'd ever see you again," she said, her voice barely above a whisper.

He crossed his arms over his chest, a smirk on his lips. "Who, me? I've got work to do."

"Right." She cleared her throat. "For Russell."

"And you."

"Me?" Eliza smiled. "Why me?"

"You need a place to hide out, right? How about I fly you to the sea pen site? You could stay in Russell's office. The visitor apartments aren't done yet, but they have water and electricity. There's even a little fridge." He put his hand out, palm up. "Unless you don't trust me."

Her chest grew hot, her blood on fire, melting everything it touched. She could hardly lift her hand to his. "I trust you."

Joey grinned. "Then come with me."

Twenty-seven

They touched onto the water and Joey circled, parking at the dock. The plane bobbed as he cut the engine, the sudden silence filled with the creaking of the floating dock.

"Do you think people might find it weird?" Eliza asked. "That I just started living in this office?"

"Honestly, no. There are always people going in and out. Tell them you're testing the water."

"Testing the water," she repeated. "Okay. Sure."

Sunlight filtered through the window and streamed onto her face as heat built inside the cockpit. Her perfume smelled of orange and bergamot.

"Should we go in?" she asked, glancing at him before turning to the door.

He snapped his eyes away. "Yeah."

It was hard to know what she was thinking. He didn't appreciate her talking to the FBI without him, especially about him, but it was a moot point. Seeing her on the dock, her lips pale and her hands shaking as she handed over her phone – it didn't matter what had been said between them. He had to help her.

Joey climbed out and stooped, tying the plane down. Eliza shut the door with a thwack that echoed in his ears.

He stood and pointed ahead. "That building there? They're almost done working on it. We'll have a meeting room and a group dining hall. There's a research facility in the next building."

She followed a few steps behind him, the metal dock bouncing with each step. "Oh."

He kept going until they reached the shore. "This way."

The path would eventually be gravel, but for now, it was mud, with cloudy puddles in the deep tire tracks.

Joey carefully stepped over them. Eliza stepped directly into one.

"You okay?" he asked, turning around.

She looked down. The mud splatters reached her knees. "Yeah."

He reached out to offer a hand but stopped himself. It was enough he'd offered her a place to stay. Eliza didn't trust him; she'd made that clear.

He kept walking. The door to the office was unlocked. Inside, directly across from the door, was a framed picture of a black wolf, a dusting of snow on its snout. A desk sat in the corner and a mini fridge hummed at its side.

In the back of the room was a pair of windows. A recliner sat facing the view of the sea, the brown leather worn light on the armrests where many had sat before.

"It's a little barren, but it'll do for now."

She nodded and set her purse on the desk.

"Did you ever answer Mackenzie?"

She shook her head.

"I should probably tell Mackenzie where you are," he said.

"Yeah." She stood at the window, her back to him.

Joey sighed. Why had she come with him if she wasn't going to talk to him?

"Do you want me to bring you some stuff? Clothes, food? A blanket?"

She cleared her throat. "That would be nice. Sure."

He waited for her to say more, but when she didn't, he shrugged. "All right then."

Joey spun, shutting the door behind him.

Sure, she'd come along, but she wasn't going to involve him. She'd cut him out of looking for the robber long ago, and now she was leaving him out even more.

He could take the hint. He wasn't wanted here. Eliza didn't trust him – not really – and she wanted nothing to do with him. As soon as his contract expired, he'd be gone. She'd never have to hear from him again.

His breath grew heavy and hot. This whole job was a mistake. He'd take whatever came up next and forget any of it had happened.

Joey ducked down to untie the plane and pulled out his phone. He could send Mackenzie a text, but would it be better for Eliza to call? They would think he'd kidnapped her.

He ran back to the office, slowing when he got to the door and heard something.

At first, he thought it was an animal – a bird, maybe. But he leaned closer, listening.

Crying. It was Eliza, sobbing and gasping and sniffing.

He knocked on the door, loudly announcing, "Hey, I forgot something."

Silence, then, "Come in!"

The door creaked as he pushed it open. "I'll leave you my phone in case you want to get in contact with anyone."

Eliza spun around. Her nose was red and her cheeks were streaked with black. Apparently, she did wear makeup.

The burning fury in his chest disappeared, as though someone had thrown salted, stinging seawater on the flame, extinguishing it in a flash.

She waved a hand. "That's really nice of you. I appreciate you doing this."

She took the cell phone from his hand.

"My password is 1-2-3-5," he said. "That'll unlock it. The battery might be a little low, but I can find a charger."

She nodded. "Thank you."

Not even a crack at how terrible of a passcode that was.

She fidgeted, her breath jagged. "You should probably go. In case anyone comes looking for me. I don't want you to get in trouble."

He stared at her, acutely aware of how loud his breathing was. His mind tumbled and his heart accelerated in his chest.

She wasn't afraid of him. She was afraid *for* him.

Joey sucked in a breath. He had to say something. "Right. I'll be in touch."

The door creaked on the way out.

. . .

He took off, the sea pen shrinking beneath him. He flew east, toward the tea shop, but he thought of the workers finishing their lunches and looking for him and turned around, pointing the plane toward Roche Harbor.

It wouldn't help Eliza to have a bunch of guys making noise and stomping around, though. He could come up with an excuse as to why they needed to be done for the day. Russell wouldn't mind, would he?

He turned east again, gripping the controls until his hands hurt.

How selfish could he be? He'd only thought of his side of things. It was reasonable for Eliza to wonder if he was the robber. Why hadn't he listened to her? Why did he have to immediately attack, to treat her like the enemy?

She hadn't even accused him of being the robber. She said she didn't care. All she wanted was for him to stay, but she knew he wouldn't.

That was what set him off. Not that she'd said it. That she was right.

He splashed to a landing, tied off the plane and ran. His feet pounded the dock, then the rocks, then the grassy hillside.

Leaving wasn't an option. He wouldn't even consider it. He had to help her.

He broke through the trees. The tea shop was straight ahead and a black SUV that had its reverse lights on.

Eliza's Granny stood outside, waving a dish rag.

He picked up his pace as Granny yelled at the SUV. "Go on now! Go home! Get out of here!"

"Hey!" He reached her and stopped, sucking in gulps of air. "Mrs. Granny Patty."

She turned her head, a smile flickering on her face. "Patty is fine."

"I ran into Eliza—"

"Shush!" She snapped at him with the towel. "Come inside. Now."

The tea shop smelled of cinnamon and the warm air soothed his lungs. Sheila was seated at a table, along with Mackenzie and Russell.

"Was that the ATF?" Joey asked.

Mackenzie narrowed her eyes. "How do you know about that?"

"I ran into Eliza. She showed me the warrant."

"Where is she?" asked Mackenzie. "What did you do with her?"

He put his hands up. "Nothing. She's safe. I flew her to the sea pen site. I thought she could hide in your office, Russell."

He nodded. "Good idea. We'll stop improvements for a bit. Tell the workers there's a permit thing."

"Is it warm enough over there?" asked Sheila. "Can you take me to her? I don't want her to be alone."

Joey nodded. "Of course. No problem."

Mackenzie stepped forward, her finger pointed at his nose. "Hang on. I've been calling her phone nonstop, but she hasn't answered. How do we know you didn't kidnap her?"

"I didn't kidnap her and I am not the robber!" Joey shouted. "The only thing that happened was I accidentally helped the robber fly away, but—"

Mackenzie poked him in the shoulder. Hard. "Go and tell those agents you know who did it and that it wasn't my sister!"

"I don't know who it was," he said. "I swear. I didn't pay attention to the guy. I thought Eliza could figure it out."

She scoffed. "I don't believe you."

"Okay, enough," Sheila said, standing up. "We need to stop arguing and find a way to help Eliza."

Patty threw the dish towel over her shoulder. "I agree."

"How do we know he's not setting us all up?" Mackenzie said.

All four faces turned and looked at Joey.

"I don't know what to tell you, but it wasn't me."

The room was quiet. Patty took a step toward him. "I believe you. I know you'll find a way to prove me right."

He forced a smile. "I will."

Patty nodded. "Lock the door. It's crunch time."

Twenty-eight

The water rippled and danced, throwing dazzling shards of light into her eyes. Eliza didn't have her sunglasses. She stared out the window anyway.

Someday soon, Lottie's black fin would break this water's surface, the spout of her breath casting rainbows in the air.

It would be spectacular. The site was already spectacular, with its red-painted buildings and sweeping views of the islands. Her mom and Russell were making it happen, and Eliza had taken it all for granted.

She should have visited more often, asked more questions. Taken more pictures. She'd never expected she might end up in jail and miss everything.

She heaved herself onto the leather recliner at the other end of the room. If she didn't get arrested soon, she'd go mad, walking these halls and thinking these thoughts.

But what was there to do? The robber had eluded everyone, and Stacy had been able to provide enough evidence to convince a judge that *she* was the one to blame.

There was no way out.

Joey's phone rang. She recognized the number as her mom's, but she was afraid of answering. The line could be tapped. They could track her here. She'd like at least one night of freedom before she was arrested.

The phone only had thirty percent battery anyway. Maybe a coded text was enough.

All is well but can't chat now. Feel like Lottie, neither here nor there.

Her mom's response came a minute later. **Got it. Hang tight, talk soon!**

Hopefully Stacy and the ATF didn't have the authority to tap every phone Eliza had ever communicated with.

She pulled the recliner back and stared at the ceiling. The wood was dark and knotted, stained a handsome brown. Eliza tried to practice her zen. The ceiling could hold the answers. Perhaps if she cleared her mind, something would come to her.

Ten minutes of staring, yet nothing.

She sat up. Joey's phone was still at thirty percent battery. Maybe it wouldn't hurt to look at things again.

The service was terribly slow, but she was able to log into Mackenzie's fake account and load Stacy's page. She clicked through the pictures, zooming in on every man, no matter how far he was in the distance. Surely Stacy's robber-lover had to appear in at least one of these hundreds of pictures?

She got through two years' worth of pictures with no sign of him or, at least, what she thought he might look like. A bold smile. A trendy haircut. Maybe winking at the camera. A man with no fear.

The battery was down to twelve percent. Eliza got up and rummaged through the desk drawers. There were papers, cough drops, and a can opener, but no phone chargers.

She sat back on the recliner and closed her eyes. A knock at the door made her jump.

"It's me!" her mom's voice called. "I've brought supplies."

"Come in!" Eliza shouted, almost falling out of the recliner as she scrambled to sit up.

The door opened. Mom came through first, her arms overflowing with a fluffy blanket and towels, a book bag strapped to her back. Mackenzie followed, reusable grocery bags weighing down each arm.

"Welcome to my new apartment," Eliza said, sweeping a hand behind her. "I have a chair and a desk."

Joey stepped into view and stood in the open doorway. He waved.

Her heart fluttered into her throat. Eliza waved back. "Thanks for bringing them."

"No problem."

Mackenzie dropped the bags onto the floor with a clank. "It's the *least* he could do."

"Mack..." Mom warned, raising an eyebrow.

Mackenzie squatted down and unloaded the bags. "I'm sure you're hungry. Granny packed four sandwiches, a bag of cookies, and a quart of soup."

Eliza laughed as Mackenzie piled everything into her arms. "That's nice, but I don't have much of an appetite."

"Granny went to talk to Margie in person," Mom said, wrapping her in a hug from behind. "We're going to figure this out. Don't worry, okay?"

"I'm not," she lied, smiling. "I wanted to call my FBI contact, Ramona, but I'm afraid to give away my location."

Mom leaned in. "I think we're okay. To be safe, I can wait to call her until we're away from here."

"I brought your laptop," Mackenzie said, pulling it from the grocery bag. "Granny insisted you needed a copy of the local islander magazine, too, so here you go."

She dropped it onto the desk with a thud. The cover had a glossy picture of the lighthouse at sunset. Eliza picked it up and flipped through the pages.

The smell of a fresh magazine was always nice. Better than whatever was floating around in the stale air of the room—old containers of takeout and grease.

Mom kept hovering. "You'll hide here as long as you need to. I'll get you a better place to sleep. Would you prefer a camping cot or a blow-up mattress?"

The magazine fell open to a story: **Beloved Gift Shop to Close after 36 Years.**

The cover image was of Grace, the woman whose wheelchair had been used in the robbery. The sun rose on the harbor in the background, its orange glow illuminating her face. She stared into the distance with a solemn expression.

"I'm going to miss it," she was quoted. "No doubt about it."

Her heart rate picked up. There was something there. Eliza kept scanning the image, her eyes searching every corner.

"Honey?" Mom asked. "Are you okay?"

She looked up from the magazine. "I didn't see it before. She was wearing sunglasses."

Joey leaned forward, craning to see the page. "Grace? The shopkeeper?"

She held up the picture and pointed. "Look at her eyes! Dark green, with flecks of brown and blue, gold around the pupil. Don't you see?"

"The robber's eyes," Joey said, voice low.

"*She's* the robber?" Mackenzie asked, holding a bunch of bananas in one hand and a quart of soup in the other. "Let's get her!"

"No, the robber was a man, but...she's involved. Or someone related to her is involved. Those were his eyes; I'm sure of it."

"See! It wasn't me!" Joey said. "Look at my eyeballs!"

"Keep your eyeballs to yourself," Mackenzie said, shooting him a look. "If I find you anywhere in her family tree, I'm going to have you arrested."

He sighed. "If I find myself in her family tree, I'll arrest myself."

Eliza read the article, hopping and skipping, unable to absorb the words. She stopped at a picture of Grace and her husband from twenty years ago.

Mrs. Donovan and her husband raised five boys while running the gift shop.

"She has five sons," Eliza said. "He has to be one of them."

Mackenzie dropped the bananas. "Are you sure about this? Aren't you feeling a little...desperate?"

"Of course I'm desperate, but I still know what I'm seeing."

"Eliza is never wrong," Joey said. His eyes were on her, and when she looked up at him, he smiled.

Butterflies took off in her stomach and got caught in her throat. "We just have to figure out which one it is. Then we can tell the FBI and be done with this."

Mom clapped her hands together. "That's a plan. Okay. We can do this."

• • •

The slow connection didn't faze her. Seated at the desk, Eliza clicked wildly on her laptop, opening tabs, searching housing and employment records, pulling pictures from every corner of the internet.

In less than thirty minutes, she found him. "This is the robber. Derek Donovan."

They gathered behind her and she clicked, bringing a video to life.

"This is one of my original poems," the man said with a smile. He cleared his throat. "Falling asleep on the train, dozing off without refrain. Will we wake at our stop? Or miss it, our worries atop? Lover, lover, fears abound – you are mine. With me, you're found."

Eliza paused the video on a close shot of the guy's face.

Joey leaned in, squinting. He was so close to her she could smell the mint from his chewing gum. If only she could get closer, close enough to feel the heat coming off his skin, close enough to know if he was still angry at her...

"Wow." Mackenzie stood with her hands on her hips. "He's a great bank robber, but a terrible poet."

"Abysmal," Mom nodded.

Eliza clicked over to another tab. "This is his son, Derek Junior. He's thirteen and lives with his mom in Topeka. According to Junior's TikTok, Dad left when he was a baby to pursue his dream of becoming an actor and yoga instructor."

Joey groaned. "He can't be a real person. He's too awful. Is he really Grace's son? She seemed so nice."

Mackenzie shrugged. "It happens. What are the other sons like?"

Eliza clicked through more tabs. "They all seem to be normal members of society, at least on the surface." She paused. "One is a bank manager at a Pebble Bay Bank."

"One out of five isn't bad," Mackenzie said, stifling a laugh. "Good thing you never had that fifth daughter, Mom. That's where it might've gone wrong."

She laughed. "All of my kids are perfect. Not a bad one in the bunch."

"I know, but the fifth..." Mackenzie scrunched her nose. "Could've been bad. Could've been a bank robber. Or a Mary Bennet."

"There is nothing wrong with Mary Bennet," Eliza said.

"She's right," Joey added. "She was a bit tedious, but she was still so young and so bright."

Eliza turned to him, eyes wide. "You're a Jane Austen fan?"

"My sister watched *Pride and Prejudice* on repeat. I've always been more of a Bingley fan myself," he said, then stopped when he caught Mackenzie's eye. "Anyway, Mary was at least curious."

"Curiously boring," Mackenzie said with a smirk.

Eliza sucked in a sharp breath.

Mom put a hand on her shoulder. "Eliza, you've *done it*. You found him."

"See? You're not a Mary," Mackenzie added. "You're definitely Elizabeth."

"Are you sure it's him?" Joey asked. He was further away from her, out of reach. "I'm not doubting you, I just – I can't believe it."

Eliza stifled a smile. "I do think it's him. His voice, his mannerisms." She dug in her pocket and pulled out a business card. "I'm going to call Ramona."

Joey lurched forward, hand outstretched. "Wait. What if they track you here? Maybe we should call for you when we get back to San Juan?"

"It can't wait. She told me to call if I heard anything else." She shook her head, already punching in the number. "At this point, I'm confident if they do arrest me, Ramona will be able to get Derek."

Her mom shifted on her feet. "You trust her that much?"

Eliza nodded. "I do. And I think this is the only way out."

The phone rang. Eliza hit speakerphone and set it down.

Ramona answered, her voice clear. "FBI, this is Agent Ramona Thomas."

She didn't hold back, telling her about the arrest warrant, hiding out, and the clues leading to Derek.

She finished with, "What do you think?"

They paused in silence until Ramona sighed. "This is impressive but, Eliza, I have to be frank with you."

Her stomach dropped. "Okay."

"An arrest warrant is serious. I'm going to do everything I can, but you need to turn yourself in."

She sucked in a breath. She should have expected it, but it still stung. "I will."

"I think we can start with..." Ramona's voice trailed off. "Could you pick Derek out of a lineup?"

"Definitely."

"Hi, Ramona. This is Eliza's mom, Sheila." She leaned over the phone, her hands clasped together. "Is this enough? For an arrest?"

She sighed. "It's not exactly evidence, so no. I can ask him to come in for questioning."

"Ask him?" Mackenzie scoffed. "You can't make him?"

"Not yet."

Eliza tried to swallow, but her throat was completely dry. The only person with enough evidence for an arrest was her.

"Go to the nearest police station," she continued, "and tell them there's a warrant for your arrest. I'll meet up with my boss and see what we can do."

"I will, thank you," Eliza said, lifting a heavy limb to end the call.

Mackenzie spoke first. "You are not turning yourself in. I get that she has to say that, but no!"

"I have to, Mack."

Mom twisted her hands together. "Why do you have to wait in *prison?* Can't you just stay here?"

Eliza sunk into the seat. "No."

"You at least have to wait until Chief Hank is in tomorrow," Mom said. "You can't go turning yourself in during the middle of the night."

What does one pack for prison? Could she bring her own toothbrush? A book? "Fine, but you guys should go. You don't want to be caught around me."

"I don't care about that." Mackenzie sighed. "I'm staying."

"Me too," Mom said.

Eliza's voice was soft but resolute. "I don't want anyone to get in trouble for being with me. And I could use some time to think."

Her mom's face twisted into a frown. There were tears in her eyes. "Are you sure?"

She forced a smile. "Yes, I'm fine. This is all going to work out. Trust me."

Mackenzie gave her a hug, squeezing her tightly. "You're right. You're too smart to go to jail."

She stole a look at Joey. He was watching her, hands in his pockets.

Would she ever see him again? If she ever got out of prison, he'd surely be gone.

He cleared his throat. "Oh." He pulled a white charging cord from his pocket. "For the phone. Forgot to give this to you."

She wanted to tell him she was sorry for what she said. Sorry she'd ever doubted him, that she ever suspected him. Sorry she wouldn't get to keep seeing his half-dimpled smile or hear his uproarious laughter. Sorry she'd never feel the warm glow of his words in her heart.

Eliza wrapped the cord around her hand. "Thanks. For everything."

He nodded and disappeared through the door.

Twenty-nine

They walked back to the plane in the dwindling light, their footsteps heavy.

"I might owe you an apology," Mackenzie said when they reached the dock. "But I don't know if I'm ready to make it yet."

He knelt to untie the plane. "Fair enough." He had no argument. He may not have robbed the bank, but he had lied to Eliza. Far worse than that, he may have broken her heart, too.

They got into the plane and he pulled in his focus.

Engage the starter. Oil pressure good.

Ramona didn't seem convinced she could bring this guy in. What did that mean for Eliza? She'd get arrested and Derek would run off with Stacy? They'd never find him.

Doors secured. Controls free and correct.

What if Joey got to Derek? What if he could compel him to talk first...

Carb heat, double check.

He had to get him to talk. Get him to turn on Stacy. But how?

Instruments set. Flaps up.

It was so like Eliza to send them away. So like her to take the fall. It was obvious to her that Derek was the robber, but would it be enough to convince a jury? Especially after Derek hired a clever attorney who could point the finger back at her?

Rudders up. Nose forward.

Eliza had looked so small, sitting in that massive leather recliner. It had taken all his strength not to run across the room, scoop her up, and fly her to safety.

They could wait out Derek's arrest in secret together. Hide away in a little Italian village. Find a cottage in the Swiss alps. A tiny apartment in Berlin.

He didn't care where it was. Only that he'd be with her.

Liftoff.

They rose higher and Joey, his heart soaring, pushed the plane as fast as it'd go.

There was no going back now.

• • •

It didn't take much to edit pictures of Joey and Stacy together – twenty-seven dollars to be exact. The guy he found to do it wanted an extra six dollars to rush the order. It was done by four that morning.

Joey flew to the mainland and printed the pictures, then flew straight to Orcas Island. He landed at The Grand Madrona Hotel docks. Patty once mentioned a friend of hers ran the place; he hoped dropping her name would be enough to keep him from getting screamed at. Luckily, no one approached him at all.

According to Eliza's research, Derek's trailer sat on a small plot of land a mile and a half from the hotel.

Joey walked up the gravel driveway to the main road and a guy leaving stopped to ask if he wanted a ride. He accepted, climbing into the blue truck.

"Headed to a friend's?" the driver asked.

"Something like that." He kept his eyes watching the road, memorizing where he'd need to run if things went south.

They stopped at the **NO TRESPASSING** sign.

"Thanks." Joey popped the door to the truck open and hopped out. A narrow dirt driveway wove uphill, into the trees. He walked on, heart thundering in his ears.

The trailer sat at the top of the hill. The top and bottom third were a grey white, the middle a yellow stripe. A door sat at the edge, the top of it bent and misshapen.

Joey knocked. He heard rustling before the door flung open. Derek stood in a white tank top, his dark curly hair flopping over his forehead.

Joey's heart skipped a beat when he saw Derek's gold-flecked eyes squinting into the rising sun.

"Can I help you?"

He took a slow breath. "I'm Joey. I need to talk to you."

Derek crossed his arms over his chest. "I don't know any Joeys."

"It's about Stacy."

His muscles stiffened. "I don't know any Stacys either. Get out of here before I call the police."

Joey put up a hand. "I wouldn't do that if I were you. Stacy might already have the police looking for you."

His face twisted. "What? Why?"

"That's what we need to talk about." Joey forced a sigh. "Do you want to get arrested right now or not?"

Derek peered over Joey's shoulder. All Joey could hear was his own breathing.

"Get inside."

The door closed with a clap, Derek slipping inside.

Joey's lungs burned like he'd just run ten miles. He took a deep breath and pulled the door open. His eyes adjusted to the warm glow of light inside the trailer. A counter straight ahead held a stack of papers. On top of that was a ukulele. The sink overflowed with empty cans, the lids standing straight up like knives.

Derek sat on a cracked blue couch. "How do you know Stacy?"

Joey reached into his pocket and pulled out the stack of glossy pictures. The one on top was of him and Stacy at a picnic. He handed them over. "I could ask you the same question."

Derek passed through the pictures, getting to the back of the stack, eyes lingering. "So she's been keeping you on the side."

"No." Joey crossed his arms over his chest. He could feel his pulse in every vein. "She's keeping *you* on the side. Stacy and I have been together for years." He shrugged. "On and off."

Derek tossed the stack of pictures onto the couch cushion next to him and shrugged. "Did you come here to fight me? You can have her."

"I'm not here to fight you. I want to get back at her."

Derek smirked and sat back. "That's fine. Leave me out of it."

"She told me about you. About the banks."

Derek leapt to his feet, his face inches away from the tip of Joey's nose. His breath was hot and smelled of sour milk. "What did you just say to me?"

"I'm telling you what she told me." Joey didn't budge. "If you don't want to hear it, I'll leave."

Derek stared, his eyes hard. He sat down. "What did she tell you?"

Joey lowered his shoulders, the muscles in his back softening. "She told me she was using you, that she was going to take the money to run away with me. She said she has all the evidence to frame you for the robberies."

He shook his head. "No. She can't. She wouldn't do that to me."

Joey held his breath. "She can and she will. She's doing it right now."

Derek snapped his head to the side. "This isn't happening." He slammed his fist into the wall. "She wouldn't do this to me!" His eyes were rimmed red, tears glimmering at the lids.

Some small, innocent part of Joey's heart sunk. It didn't feel good to trick a guy like this.

The rest of his heart, beating fast in his chest, reminded him that Stacy and Derek were happy to send Eliza to prison in their place.

He didn't feel so bad.

"I didn't think she would lie to me, either. It's bad, man. I know." Joey raised his hand slowly and placed it on Derek's shoulder.

Derek buried his face in his hands. "I should've seen this coming."

"There was no way for you to know. But you can turn her in. Let her take the fall."

Derek sat up, shaking his head. "I can't. I love her. You don't get it."

"She told me she's going to turn you in today. She said she was going to prove to me that this was all fake."

His jaw dropped. "There's no way."

"That's what she told me. If she gets to them first, explains her side..." Joey shrugged. "It's going to be hard for you to convince them she's lying. She's an agent, man. They're going to believe whatever she says."

Derek sat back against the couch and pulled a cigarette out of his pocket. He lit it, taking a deep drag. "What do I need to do?"

Thirty

Sunlight crept into the office and the warm glow filled Eliza's eyelids. She stirred under the blanket, pulling it over her chin before yawning and opening her eyes.

Her night in the old recliner had gone by quickly. She'd had no dreams, just darkness and rest. She rose, stretching, and picked up the towel and bag of toiletries her mom had brought the night before. Slipping on her shoes, she headed into the chilled morning air.

Two buildings down from the office were the nearly finished short-stay rooms. She snuck into the first one, her footsteps echoing in the empty space. There was no furniture yet but, according to Joey, the hot water heaters had been replaced the week before and were in working order.

She turned on the shower and stood beneath it until the mirrors fogged with steam.

After getting dressed, she returned to the office and packed her things. There was a text waiting from her mom.

Good morning, sweetheart! I hope you had some rest. Let me know when you're awake and I'll come by!

The birds sang and the waves crashed. She wouldn't be stuck in prison forever. She believed that. She had to.

No need. I'm calling the Chief now. Don't worry! It's all going to work out!

She hit send, then immediately called the San Juan County Police non-emergency number. A woman answered.

She took a shaky breath. "Hi. My name is Eliza Dennet and there is a warrant out for my arrest."

It came out just like she'd practiced.

"Hold please," said the flat voice. "I'll transfer you."

The line clicked and Chief Hank answered. "Eliza! I was told to expect your call."

"Hi, Chief. This is Eliza Dennet and I have a warrant—"

He cut her off. "I know. I talked to your Granny this morning. She said you're a rule follower."

"Uh – yes, I guess so." She hesitated. She'd planned for more resistance, or at least more urgency. Was it every day people turned themselves in? "Can I give you my coordinates? I'm on Stuart Island. I'm not quite sure how to get back..."

Taking Joey's phone was perhaps not her brightest idea. She'd forgotten she'd need a ride this morning.

The thought of seeing him made her stomach flip. When he'd thrown her phone into the ocean, she'd thought for a split second they might run away together. The thrill that had run through her then...

"How about I come pick you up?" Chief said.

"That would be great."

"I'll be there in half an hour."

"Thank you."

She put on her coat and waited at the dock, her legs folded beneath her. Sea otters rolled and splashed at the edge of the shore and a pair of seagulls bickered over a fish. It would have been a perfect place to meditate if she weren't waiting to be arrested.

The police boat first appeared as a silver spot in the distance. Eliza stood and waved. "Over here!"

Chief Hank pulled up to the dock with a hard frown on his face. "Eliza Dennet?"

"Hi, Chief. Yes, it's me."

He removed his black aviator sunglasses and squinted at her. "I'm under strict orders to take you for breakfast before placing you under arrest."

She shook her head. "That's okay, I don't need—"

"*Strict* orders," he said firmly, a smile crossing his face. "Hop on."

"If you're the Chief Deputy Sheriff," she asked, carefully stepping onto the boat, "who are you taking orders from?"

He grinned, starting the engine. "I'll give you one guess."

They took off and Eliza zipped her jacket shut. Chief Hank pointed out spots of note – a rock where he'd jumped onto an unmoored boat during a storm; the remnants of a house fire where the family goat alerted the family late at night and everyone had gotten out safely.

"I have to say," he told her, hands in the pockets of his black coat, "I'm impressed with how you solved that bank robbery. You could have a promising career as a detective."

Eliza turned to him, laughing. "You can't be serious."

He kept his eyes straight ahead. "I am."

She turned back. They were gliding past another island – she wasn't sure which one. The shores were smooth and graceful, bowing in and out of the sea. "Thanks for that."

They landed on Lopez Island and had breakfast at a little restaurant where everyone knew Chief. One woman spotted him through the window and came in to yell at him about her chickens disappearing.

"There's a chicken thief on the island and no one is taking me seriously," she said before storming out.

Her plate of scrambled eggs, pancakes, and bacon glistened with butter and syrup. She tried to avoid looking at it, taking small bites until Chief was done eating.

On their way out, after they'd finished their meal, the chicken lady caught them again. "You aren't going to believe this, but my two missing chickens are back! I guess the thief heard you were in town."

He nodded. "I guess so."

She handed him a half carton of eggs. "For your troubles, Chief."

Eliza watched her walk away, the hood of her jacket bouncing with every step. "Do you think she's the thief?"

"I think her chickens like to go for walks," he said with a smile. "But you already knew that, didn't you, Detective?"

Eliza smiled. "Is it time for me to be arrested yet? We've had breakfast."

"What, are you in a hurry?" He raised an eyebrow. "I need to talk to the deputies here. Check on morale. Make some calls."

What was the point of her trying to rush him? Granny had clearly gotten to him. "No problem. I've got all the time in the world."

After talking to the local deputies, they borrowed a cruiser and investigated a citizen complaint. A man on the eastern side of the island claimed his neighbor was throwing paint onto his deck. Upon investigation, Chief Hank and Eliza determined the paint was, in fact, bird poop.

"Another case closed," Chief said, dusting his hands off when they got back to the car.

Eliza smiled. "This is fun and all, but I'd really like to be arrested now. Can you please stop stalling and put me out of my misery?"

"I don't know what you're talking about." He started the car. "We'll go back to the boat—how's that?"

Eliza never thought she'd be relieved about getting arrested, but on the boat ride to San Juan Island, she was finally able to relax. She sat peacefully on the boat, looking out on the water as the sun warmed her face.

She was doing what she was supposed to do. She trusted the FBI would do the same and it would all work out.

Unless, of course, Stacy and Derek found out what she'd been up to and managed to plan a daring escape...

She stood from her seat. There was no point in thinking like that. She'd done all she could do. The rest was out of her hands.

They arrived in Friday Harbor and walked to the police station.

"You're the least wily criminal I've ever had to deal with," Chief said.

"Really?" she frowned. "I thought I was pretty clever, hiding at the sea pen site."

He scoffed. "That would been the first place I would've looked if I'd ever gotten that warrant on you."

"You haven't seen it yet?"

"Fax machine was unplugged. Figure that." He shrugged, pulling the door to the police station open. "After you."

She walked in and Chief Hank followed. He stopped to speak to the secretary, then two of the deputies, then a concerned citizen who wanted to report goats grazing on his property.

"I won't have it, Hank! I just won't," the man said, stomping his foot.

Chief nodded, pulling a notepad and pen from his pocket. "Where again did you say this was?"

Eliza leaned in, looking at the notepad. In the center of the page was a sketch of a goat.

She pulled away, biting her lip.

Finally, they got into his office. "Take a seat."

She did and he sat across from her. Chief sighed, typing on his computer keyboard one finger at time.

He clicked here and there, then sat back and sighed again before punching the red button on his desk phone and dialing a number.

A voice came through on speakerphone. "Agent Burns."

"Hey, it's Chief Deputy Sheriff Hank Kowalski over on San Juan Island. I had a warrant for an Eliza Dennet come through yesterday. I have apprehended the fugitive, but I can't seem to find the warrant in my system."

"Ah, hang on." Clicking. Typing. "It's been canceled. You can release her."

"Thank you."

He lifted the phone's receiver and dropped it with a click. "Looks like you're free to go." A phone rang outside the office, the hollow sound filling the room.

Eliza stared at him. "What?"

"I expected you'd be relieved, but I can't tell you how relieved *I* am." He sat back, resting his hands on his belly. "Your Granny said she would gut me like a fish if I arrested you."

A cold feeling expanded from her stomach and out to her limbs. "Does that mean they got Derek? Is there enough evidence to arrest him?"

Hank shrugged and put his hands up in the air. "No idea! All I know is I get to live another day and not get baked into one of your Granny's fish pies."

Eliza put her hand over her mouth. "I can't believe this."

"Would you like a ride home?" he asked.

She'd taken up enough of his time. "No. Thank you, though. I'll just call my mom if that's okay."

He nodded. "Sure."

There was nothing quite like telling a police officer about needing to call her mom to make her feel like a giddy schoolgirl.

She punched in the number and her mom answered with a shaky, "Hello?"

She leapt out of her chair. "Mom! I'm coming home!"

. . .

After much squealing, they hung up and Eliza went outside to wait. It took six minutes for her ride to get there.

"I can't believe you turned yourself in!" Mom yelled through the open window when she pulled up to the police station. "But I'm so happy we can put this all behind us."

Eliza grinned, hopping into the passenger seat. "I know and I'm sorry. I didn't want anyone else to get involved."

"I wanted to fly up there as soon as I got your message, but I couldn't find Joey."

"Oh really? Where is he?"

"I don't know! No one has heard from him all day. Russell was about to rent a water taxi to come and get you."

Something tightened in her chest. "Do you think he's okay?"

She waved a hand. "I'm sure he's fine."

"Is the plane at the dock?"

Mom tapped her chin with her finger. "No. It's missing, too."

Eliza looked down at her hands. She shouldn't be surprised he'd taken off after all this craziness, and yet...she was.

She'd held onto hope that maybe, just *maybe,* he'd forgive her for what she'd said.

She stared out the window and let out a breath.

It didn't matter. Even if he had forgiven her, it didn't mean he wanted to change. There was no use trying to change him – or anyone. Joey was someone who had to run away. She had to let him, for her own sanity.

They pulled into the tea shop and Granny came running out in her apron.

"You did it!" She hugged Eliza so tightly she couldn't breathe.

"I did," she squeaked.

"Now did Hank arrest you? Because if he did –"

"No, Granny. He stalled for hours. I got a police tour of the island. He even took me to breakfast."

"It better have been somewhere good," Granny said, scowling.

Eliza laughed. "It was."

"Shall we go inside?" Mom said with a smile.

Mackenzie walked out of the kitchen with a teapot in her hands. "My fugitive sister has returned!"

Eliza took a bow. "Thank you. Yes, I am back."

"Good." She set the teapot down. "What do you think you'll do with the reward money?"

She laughed. "I don't care about the money. I'm just glad not to be in jail."

"You certainly deserve to get the reward!" Granny said, taking a seat. "If it weren't for you, Stacy and that man would've gotten away with it."

Mackenzie laughed. "If it weren't for you darned kids..." She pulled out her phone. "Look at this! I just got a news alert."

They leaned in and Mackenzie played a video with the headline **DISGRACED ATF AGENT ARRESTED IN CONNECTION WITH STRING OF ROBBERIES.**

Eliza gasped. Stacy was front and center, arms handcuffed behind her back, making a sour face at the reporters shouting questions.

"I thought they said there wasn't enough evidence to arrest her?" Eliza said.

"Guess they figured it out," Mackenzie said airily. "What do you want to do with your freedom?"

She smiled. "I think...I just want to enjoy a cup of tea."

Mackenzie locked the door to the tea shop and hung a handwritten sign: **Closed today for a family emergency.**

For the next two hours, they drank tea and laughed and ate cookies. Eliza was about to open the new peach green tea they'd ordered when they heard a banging at the door.

"I'll get it," Mackenzie said, leaping out of her chair.

She returned a moment later. "Mom? Granny? I think we're needed back at the house."

They shot each other a look and got up without another word.

"Where are you going?" Eliza narrowed her eyes. "What are you planning?"

Mackenzie pretended to zip her lips closed and winked. They disappeared through the back door and Eliza stood, staring at the mess of a table they'd left behind – napkins, half-drunk tea, and crumbs.

Maybe they were making dinner. Or maybe –

"Hey!"

She spun around.

Joey.

The air left her lungs. He was dressed as though he'd stepped out of her memory, wearing the same thing he'd worn the day they met. The black LL Bean bomber jacket. A gray shirt, dark jeans, and white Nike sneakers with a red swoosh.

The only thing missing were his RayBan sunglasses, which he'd left with her at the sea pen site.

"I have something for you," he said, holding a finger up. He slipped out the front door and reappeared holding an enormous piece of cardboard almost as wide as he was tall.

Eliza gasped, covering her mouth with her hands. It was a giant check. Handwritten on the check was her name, along with an attempt at a cursive one hundred thousand dollars.

"This isn't the official check," he said, frowning. "I picked it up at a novelty store in Seattle. But I did confirm with the bank that they'll be crediting you for catching the robber."

She had both hands on her face. "*Joey!*"

He looked down at the check and smiled. "My handwriting's not the best, but I think it gets the idea across."

"Where have you been?" she blurted, dropping her hands.

He set the check down and propped it against a chair. "I've been trying to find a way to show you I'm sorry. And to tell you..." He cleared his throat. "Tell you how much you mean to me."

Eliza leaned in, squinting at his scrawled handwriting on the check. "You're the one who wrote 'aka Elizabeth Bennet' on here?"

"Yeah." He opened his mouth, then shut it. "Because 'I fell in love with you the first day I met you' wouldn't fit."

Her limbs tingled, her fingers almost numb. "I think I need to take a seat."

Joey rushed forward and pulled out a chair, the wooden legs screeching across the floor. "Please."

She sat down, the room spinning away.

He took a seat across from her. "I was a jerk."

She put a hand up. "I accused you of being the bank robber. I get it."

"You never believed that," he said with a half smile.

She couldn't tear her eyes away from that smile. "No. I didn't."

"You were right, though. I was planning to leave. Fly away, as you eloquently put it."

"Is that eloquent?"

"It was, and kinder than I deserve. I've been running away for years." He sighed. "Hiding, really."

Those beautiful green eyes. "Hiding from what?"

He looked down, then back up, locking his gaze. "At first, it was thrilling to go to these places. Life was an adventure, but after a while, it all started to blend together. I wasn't excited anymore. I wasn't scared."

A smile curled on her lips. "You like being scared?"

"I thought I did, but meeting you scared me more than anything; I wouldn't admit it to myself. I just wanted to run."

She laughed. "So cliché."

"Oh, like you aren't? A brilliant, beautiful prodigy with self-deprecating humor and a knack for catching criminals?"

Her breath hung heavy in her chest. "Beautiful, you say?"

Joey smiled and put his hands on hers. "Yes, beautiful."

"Hm." His hand was so warm and so soft. Her mind went fuzzy and all the muscles in her body seemed to melt.

He cleared his throat. "I need to tell you I saw Derek this morning."

She tilted her head. "Derek?"

"I convinced him I was dating Stacy and she was setting him up to take the fall."

She gasped. "How did you do that?"

"Just a few photoshopped pictures." Joey shrugged. "He's a hothead. It didn't take much. He turned himself in to get a better deal. Ratted her out."

Her mouth dropped open. "Joey! What if he'd tried to hurt you?"

"I'm not afraid of old wanna-be poet Derek."

"But—"

He squeezed her hand. "It was worth it. You're safe."

Her face grew hot and tears pricked her eyes. "Thanks," she said, her voice barely above a whisper.

He flashed a smile. "I had this idea I wasn't cut out for love. That I'd tried it once and it showed me I was supposed to fly solo." He shook his head. "I really believed it, and I don't know what makes me more of a dope – that or giving rides to criminals."

Eliza scrunched her nose. "Probably the criminal thing."

"Yeah." He sighed. "I was wrong, but I didn't know it until I met you."

"You saw me in here and thought, 'She'll catch the guy I gave a ride to, I just know it.'"

Eliza smiled at him as he shook his head. Joey put his other hand on top of hers. "Yeah, but I don't care about any of that. It was just a cover. An excuse to spend more time with you."

"Ah. So I didn't have to pretend to be the perfect investigation partner?"

He leaned in. "I just like you, Eliza. I didn't fall in love with you because you're perfect. I fell in love with you because you're you. Everything about you is enough."

Enough. With one word, a dam inside her chest cracked, the sound of thick timber giving way.

The idea she didn't have to have a perfect career, a perfect body, a perfect life before someone could love her?

Tears burst from her eyes and spilled onto her cheeks. "I don't know what to say."

"You don't have to say anything." He pulled her closer, kissing the top of her head.

Eliza leaned into him, closing her eyes and resting on his firm chest. "You smell nice."

He laughed. "So do you."

She looked up at him. "You know, you're going to have to do better than that for our first kiss."

He grinned down at her. "My apologies."

She closed her eyes. His lips fluttered onto hers and the room disappeared around them.

Epilogue

The bank held a ceremony for Eliza at the San Juan Island branch. Mackenzie attended, along with the other two Dennet sisters, Emma and Shelby (Lydia and Kitty Bennet, respectively).

It was no easy task convincing her little sisters to make the trip. In typical Lydia and Kitty fashion, the youths had lofty summer plans with visions of beaches and late nights out—coming to a regional bank on a Saturday afternoon was not part of it.

Mackenzie really had to push. "It's not every day your sister wins a hundred thousand dollars," she told them. Eventually, she escalated to, "Now Eliza's the only one who has any money, so if you run into trouble, you're going to need her."

It worked, and she was only stretching the truth a little. It would have been a hundred thousand, except Eliza had insisted on splitting the reward with Joey.

Mackenzie was ready to hold this against him until she'd learned he'd risked his life to trick Derek into confessing.

"Still," she teased Joey as they sipped on lemonade while Eliza chatted with a local reporter. "Half?"

He laughed. "I agree with you. I'm just glad I'll always have you to keep me honest."

"Always," Mackenzie said with a nod.

She wasn't sure if she wanted to move to the island, but the longer she stayed, the more comfortable it became. Her old life faded like an outdated ship in the distance. A job that had once suffocated her was suddenly nothing but a fading dot on the horizon.

She hadn't closed a sale since she'd arrived, either. It felt surprisingly great. It became a game to her – how long could she drag it out before they'd fire her?

Mackenzie wanted to let it evolve naturally. The only move she initiated was reaching out to Steve's fiancée Addy.

There was a chance Addy had been duped by Steve, too, and she deserved to know what kind of man she was marrying.

It took her a few weeks, but Mackenzie penned a succinct email explaining her relationship with Steve, even going as far to provide pictures in case he tried to weasel his way out of admitting the truth.

Addy's response was swift and brief.

"I won. You lost. Get over it, Mackenzie." She signed it with a picture of her smiling and holding her ringed finger up to the camera.

The picture made Mackenzie laugh out loud. She'd felt guilty all this time, worrying that Addy would be just as blindsided, that she should've told her sooner.

At least, after sending the email, she knew Steve had picked the right woman.

• • •

After saying their goodbyes at the bank, everyone headed to the tea shop for Granny's after party. They were lined up outside for the potato sack races Granny had insisted on when Mackenzie's phone rang.

"Excuse me," Mackenzie said, tossing her potato sack to Shelby. "I'll be back to beat the winner in a minute."

She stepped away, facing the seaside, the laughter behind her muffled by the wind. "Hello?"

"Hi, Mackenzie? This is Alana with HR. How are you doing?"

Here it was. The moment she'd been waiting for. "Good. How are you?"

"I'm doing well, but I do have some difficult news."

She smiled. "Do you."

"Your manager Steve has some concerns about you abiding by the company's code of conduct. After talking with us, we thought it would be a good idea to build a process improvement plan together."

She shut her eyes. Wouldn't they just fire her already? Was he really going to try to code-of-conduct her out of there?

"Alana, did you know I was the highest grossing salesperson last year?"

"Yes," she stammered, "which is why we're dedicated to finding a way through this."

A bird swooped over her head, hovering with wings outstretched on the ocean breeze. The sea, calm save for whispers of wind, lay directly ahead of her. Two orange kayaks milled past, floating the day away.

The last rays of sunlight soaked into her skin. Mackenzie looked up and smiled.

This wasn't going to be a difficult decision after all.

"That won't be necessary," Mackenzie said. "The only violation of the code of conduct was my romantic relationship with Steve. I'm happy to send you proof, along with my formal resignation."

"Oh. Oh my," Alana said.

"Please note he was my manager at the time. Use that information however you wish. Have a nice day!"

She hung up the phone and looked up. Eliza waved at her, a red potato sack in her hand. "You and me, sis!" she yelled.

The sea stretched impossibly far ahead, the edges hazy where the sky and water met, a stretch of boundless promise.

Mackenzie grinned and broke into a run, the wind lifting her outstretched arms.

The Next Chapter

Introduction to *A Spot at Starlight Beach*

Love triangles happen when you least expect—or want—them.

Mackenzie Dennet is ready to put her past behind her. Especially her romantic past. Moving to San Juan Island and working on the sea pen project was a perfect way to focus on building a happy, uncomplicated future for herself. It would've worked, too.

If she hadn't met *them*.

Cameron, an ambitious salesman with confidence for days, and Liam, a soulful, brooding artist, are complete opposites. In fact, the only thing they have in common is their interest in *her*...and the way they both tempt her to give love a second chance.

At some point, she knows she'll have to make a choice. And no matter who she chooses, someone will end up broken hearted.

All she can do now is hope it won't be her. Again.

A Spot at Starlight Beach is the third book in the Spotted Cottage Series. Get your copy now and get ready for a fun and romantic tale!

Reader's Newsletter

Sign up for my reader's newsletter and get a free cookie recipe perfected by Eliza herself, plus tea recommendations!

Visit: https://mailchi.mp/565dfd3070b5/aspotoftea to sign up.

About the Author

Amelia Addler writes always sweet, always swoon-worthy romance stories and believes that everyone deserves their own happily ever after.

Her soulmate is a man who once spent five weeks driving her to work at 4AM after her car broke down (and he didn't complain, not even once). She is lucky enough to be married to that man and they live in Pittsburgh with their little yellow mutt. Visit her website at AmeliaAddler.com or drop her an email at amelia@AmeliaAddler.com.

Also by Amelia...

The Spotted Cottage Series
The Spotted Cottage by the Sea
A Spot of Tea
A Spot at Starlight Beach

The Westcott Bay Series
Saltwater Cove
Saltwater Studios
Saltwater Secrets
Saltwater Crossing
Saltwater Falls
Saltwater Memories
Saltwater Promises
Christmas at Saltwater Cove

The Orcas Island Series
Sunset Cove
Sunset Secrets
Sunset Tides
Sunset Weddings
Sunset Serenade

Made in the USA
Monee, IL
12 September 2024

65394407R00146